Murder in Snowflake Village

The Morgan Sisters Sleuthing Club

Iris Wardlow

RED OAK

PUBLISHING HOUSE

Published in the United States by Red Oak Publishing House, LLC.

Library of Congress Catalog-in-Publication data available upon request.

ISBN (hardcover):979-8-9937932-0-7

ISBN (paperback): 979-8-9937932-1-4

ISBN (eBook): 979-8-9937932-2-1

Cover design by Chrise Wheeler & Katie Wheeler

Printed in the United States of America

First Edition: November 2025

To my identical twin daughters,

Katie and Chrise,

my everything

Prologue

The gentleman had hunted his quarry for months and believed his preparations were flawless. He would make his move before the locals departed. He spied the target weaving in and out of the jolly melee, unaware of his watchful gaze. He was very prudent to remain undetected, even though he was sure his mark had no idea who he was. Mistake number one.

Although his target was not only savvy but quite devious, he knew he was the better player in this diabolical game. He had never failed in any of his previous pursuits. Not once. He was a professional. He knew he would win. Mistake number two-never underestimate your opponent.

The gentleman was a patient hunter, always letting the opportunity present itself. He stealthily maneuvered himself away from the gaiety as his mark separated from the revelers and ventured outside. He quietly followed the prey toward a small supply shed. Perfect, he thought, and proceeded to make his final move. He now knew exactly how it would all go down. His pulse accelerated as he envisioned the face-to-face confrontation that would, at last, end the charade.

"Mr. Bartholomew," came an unexpected voice from the dark. "So nice to finally meet you."

It was not the face he was expecting. Strike three. He's out.

1

Snowflake Village

It was just turning dusk in the quaint Welsh village of North Falls, Ohio, as a slight breeze blew the remaining autumn leaves across the deserted walkway. There was just a twinge of chill in the air as the lampposts began flickering a golden glow, reflected in the storefront windows. Not far away, the community park was aglow with the remaining hints of late fall, as the trees shuddered at the loss of their leaves, stolen by the breeze and swept away to parts unknown. As Thanksgiving memories were once again stored away; turkeys, pilgrims, and pumpkins were being replaced with cozy holiday adornments.

Elizabeth (Morgan) Evans felt as if she had just stepped into a storybook. As she meandered down the beautifully lit street, her thoughts returned to how the village would transform into a magical realm of reds, greens, and golds, along with flourishes of holly, candy canes, extravagant embellishments, and the enticing aromas of the holiday season. Her festive thoughts were abruptly interrupted as she returned to the disturbing reason for her evening stroll.

Elizabeth was a retired schoolteacher, but not the average retiree. She dressed as though she just stepped out of a fashion magazine, and not just one for frumpy seniors. She was trim, loads of fun, and always active. She was rather tall with raven hair, cut short but trendy, sapphire eyes with just a twinkle of mischief, and creamy skin (Welsh characteristics she inherited from her mother). Elizabeth was a kind woman who always treated whomever she was conversing with as though that person were the most important soul in the world; her students included. Everyone looked up to Mrs. Evans.

She taught English at the local high school for thirty years and was known as the North Falls glamorous grammarian. She was constantly asked if she would write an article for the local newspaper, the *North Falls Standard,* or proofread a letter from the school's administration before it hit the public's eye. She never refused or complained about the extra duties added to her already full schedule; however, she had no qualms about saying "No" when her boundaries were crossed.

Her former students would be the first to voice that she was a disciplinarian. Her classes were rewarding and rich with information they would use their entire lives. She had a knack for bringing out the best in all of them, and they admired her impartiality. Elizabeth treated everyone the same. Amusingly, everyone thought they were her favorite.

Tonight she sported a bright red cashmere coat topped off with a resplendent holiday scarf that screamed, "I'm expensive" and "Christmas is here!" Elizabeth looked rather young for her age and acted accordingly. Everyone wanted to be her friend, and she had a plethora of them. Her closest comrades were her older sisters: Beryl (Morgan) Thomas, Peg (Morgan) Lewis, and Grace (Morgan) Davis, and, of course, her identical twin daughters, Eva (pronounced Ev-a) and Ava, who would be returning from California for the holidays. Elizabeth was ecstatic.

She had not seen her daughters for months, and even though they talked daily, she was missing them a great deal. Although she kept busy, there was always a part of her counting down the days as the holidays approached.

The Evans twins, creative minds with an entrepreneurial spirit and a sharp eye for business, were deeply involved in a project rapidly gaining momentum. They operated within a fiercely competitive, fast paced industry, where grueling hours, unpredictable travel, and relentless deadlines left little room for anything else.

Eva and Ava had blue eyes and blond hair, but they inherited their smooth skin, facial shape, and sweetheart lips from their mother. Except for Elizabeth's dark hair, they could almost pass for triplets. Eva and Ava were, as their grandfather would have said, "very fair to look upon." The Welsh do not dish out personal compliments of vanity, so in translation, their grandfather thought they were "easy on the eyes." There was no bragging from the Morgans either. "If you've done something worth bragging about, let someone else tell it, not you."

The twins were reared, as was their mother, in the ancient rhythms of their Welsh bloodline, their souls steeped in the steadfast morals, values, and quiet standards handed down like heirlooms and nurtured tenderly by their grandmother. Elizabeth's pace slowed as she approached the historic town hall, its high arching windows casting a calm glimmering light into the deepening dusk, a sharp contrast to the raging storm of opinions that were, undoubtedly, waiting inside.

Tensions had been simmering all week. The village's business community was sharply divided over a proposed expansion, a new shopping mall, complete with a luxury apartment complex.

While some embraced the change, others felt protective in retaining the town's unique charm.

And then there were the final details for this year's Christmas parade theme, "Snowflake Village," dangling like forgotten garlands, leaving the community's seasonal story incomplete.

Christmas should be the best part of the year! Grumpy and difficult folks were not tolerated by Elizabeth who was a firm believer in getting one's voice heard without spewing invectives. It was all about working together as a community and making decisions that would enhance village life. Elizabeth didn't reject change; it was simply that some things she preferred to remain the same. Therefore, Elizabeth was adamantly against the new building sites because, as everyone suspected, more projects would follow, changing the ambience and structure of the community. She loved North Falls just the way it was, with its old-world glamour, specialized local shops, and Victorian lampposts lining the pristine streets right out of a Currier and Ives print. This was a special place filled with hard working, kind-hearted folks and small-town charm. Ah, there was no other place like it.

North Falls was originally settled in the 1800s by Welsh immigrants, looking for employment and a location that reminded them of the rolling hills of Wales. The Jones side of the sisters' family came from northern Wales and were coal miners. The Morgan clan immigrated from Cardiff, where they were highly educated doctors and teachers.

Not everyone in North Falls is of Welsh descent, but those that are have a persnickety attitude toward those who don't.

After three decades of teaching, Elizabeth had learned plenty of mediating experience, but there was something disconcerting about the shopping mall conflict that had contaminated the season's joyous spirit and alerted her that something strange was percolating. As her uneasiness intensified, Elizabeth pushed open the heavy wooden door and stepped into the fray.

The meeting was yet to be underway, as Elizabeth removed her Christmas scarf and carefully pulled it through the arm of her glamorous coat. She meticulously hung her outerwear on the end of the coat rack so it wouldn't get jostled and looked for some familiar faces to share in what was sure to be a rambunc-tious meeting. She was not to be disappointed.

***

"Last night's meeting was absolutely ridiculous with all that unnecessary drama," complained Peg. "Hell's bells, everyone knows that mall is going down." Peg Lewis, owner of the Bibliophile, the local bookshop, was loved by all who knew her. She was known for her vivacious personality and humorous comments, but it was not wise to underestimate her. Peg Lewis had a feisty side. In fact, there were times when she could be quite blunt, even hurtful. Peg was plump and rather busty, who dieted frequently with no visual results. Her complexion was milky smooth, which accentuated her dark hair and deep gray eyes. Peg was a beauty and quite the comic.

"I thought Ollie and Curtis were going to fist fight right there in the hall! Oh, that was so upsetting!" Grace exclaimed, a former elementary school teacher and present owner of Grace's Elegant Antiques and Furnishings. Grace Davis was the epitome of charm, and her name suited her to a T. She was quiet and thoughtful, but once she gave her opinion, it was always profound and honest. Everyone in the village had approached her at one time or another to garner her point of view for much needed guidance. Grace was respected by the entire community, and no one ever said a disparaging word against her. Grace did have one slight flaw. She was obsessed with her weight. She was a perfect size six and dressed immaculately and expensively, catching the best sales as soon as the signs went up, alerting a discount in price. If she gained an ounce, she survived on diet soda and black coffee until the blasted pound gave up the ghost. Talk about tenacious, that was Grace.

Grace was not quite the beauty Peg and Elizabeth were, but she was, in fact, a handsome woman. Her face, although not as wrinkled as Beryl's, radiated an intense refinement. Her eyes were a pale blue that went well with her hair she religiously dyed a soft, tinted blond to hide any gray that chose to peek through. She was very conscientious of her appearance, taken from the Morgan side of the family. She, too, possessed the quality of magnetically pulling friends to her. It was not a surprise that Grace was even popular during her high school years. She was selected captain of the girls' basketball team all four years and senior homecoming queen.

"Very 'un-Santa-like' for Ollie," chimed in Beryl.

Curtis Hughes, a tall, distinguished man with a sexy head of hair, with just a hint of silver at his temples, was the president of the North Falls Community Bank. Curtis was trim and quite the looker in his slim-fitting business suits. In fact, most women in the village thought he was the bachelor to be snagged, and living in one of the most exclusive neighborhoods didn't hurt either. Wow, what a house!

Ollie Williams, on the other hand, was the perfect paragon of Kris Kringle. Ollie was not only a dead ringer for Mr. Claus but had the perfect "Ho, Ho, Ho!" All the children loved him. Ollie was a retired custodian at North Falls Elementary School and had played Ole Saint Nick for decades. He was beloved by each and every staff member, student, and parent; so when Ollie and good-looking Curtis almost came to blows, a sudden silence descended over the town hall. Team Hunk or Team Santa...how would the village choose?

The Morgan sisters, as everyone referred to them, were meeting for a late lunch at the Sugar Bowl, owned and operated by Beryl Thomas, a stereotypical grandmother in her late seventies with salt-and-pepper hair who wore neat dresses, protected by her homemade aprons. Beryl wouldn't be caught dead wearing pants! Her home cooking was legendary, and just the mention of her name caused community members' mouths to start watering. Beryl was kind, wise, and very old fashioned, with a deep wrinkled face she inherited from her *mam-gu*, (pronounced mam-gee, meaning grandmother or beloved mother) and a beatific smile. Elizabeth always loved hearing Beryl quote their mother. "It takes just as long to put on something neat as it does to put on something sloppy, so put on something neat!" and "Old fashion never goes out of style!" Seren Jones Morgan will always live on through Beryl.

The Sugar Bowl was located on the main thoroughfare of the tiny town. Just like in olden times, there was a bell that announced a new customer as it gently tinkled to welcome anyone who was in search of a delicious meal at a reasonable price. The outside was antiquated brick, which followed through to the interior. The walls were adorned with tasteful art from local artists and were for sale. "I like to help out our talented locals anyway I can," Beryl liked to say. She was also known to give away food to the less fortunate.

The artistic touches were highlighted by soft, homey lighting that made one want to remain in the relaxing atmosphere long after the last bite was eaten. Elizabeth's favorite item was the fish sandwich, rolled in Beryl's secret breading, deep fried to a golden brown, and smothered in homemade tartar sauce. People came from miles around to taste Beryl's renowned cooking and experience down-home hospitality. Everyone went away stuffed, happy, and planning their next visit to "Delicious Land."

"Elizabeth, dear, you've been exceedingly quiet this morning," remarked Beryl mildly. "Is there something bothering you?" Beryl was always a bit intuitive, being a Pisces, and was empathetic to all who were lucky enough to know her. She was the gem of North Falls.

"Are you still upset that someone nicked your scarf?" asked Peg impatiently, concluding that the scarf was gone, let it go, move on.

"Eva and Ava took me after-Christmas shopping last year when I eyed that scarf. It was the most gorgeous thing I had ever seen, but far more than I was willing to pay, even on sale. So when we got back to the car, they surprised me with it. That made it doubly special. I've been waiting a whole year to wear it, so, yes, I'm very upset." Elizabeth was hoping for some sympathy, not a reprimand for her lax disregard of a cherished token. It wasn't just a scarf, it was much more, and the thought that someone had deliberately snatched it from her was a cruel betrayal of her trust. The loss struck her deeply.

"Well, why didn't you stick it in your purse then?" inquired Peg, somewhat exasperated over the whole overblown situation.

"I've been kicking myself all morning for not doing just that. I mean who would steal a woman's Christmas scarf?" lamented Elizabeth, still refusing to believe that it was truly snitched. "I just can't comprehend what type of person would do such a thing!"

"People didn't act like that in my day. Why, we never used to lock our doors when we left the house," said Beryl, the eldest sister, leaning back with a look of utter disgust coloring her face.

"I wouldn't even think of walking off and leaving my house open today. It's a shame how society has regressed."

"Oh yes, I remember those golden days, and I so long for them again," stated Grace rather dreamily.

As the sisters finished their lunch and continued their conversation, they were totally oblivious that someone, close by, was listening intently to their every word, and that eavesdropper knew exactly who had stolen Elizabeth's scarf.

2

An Unexpected Meeting

When Elizabeth left the meeting last night, she was terribly disappointed that her scarf went missing, especially after she had been so careful to leave it securely positioned in her sleeve. She announced the theft immediately, and everyone available gave the hall a thorough look. The mayor scoured the stage, Councilman Lloyd searched the foyer, the ladies auxiliary checked the kitchen and bathrooms, while everyone else peeked in closets and corners. The scarf was nowhere to be seen. It then became painfully clear. Someone had deliberately robbed her of the posh scarf.

Exiting the Sugar Bowl, Elizabeth's spirits were at an all-time low, especially after Peg's cool dismissive attitude. She took the short walk down the block to Leave Me in Stitches, the local cross-stitch shop. This was one of her favorite shops in all North Falls!

The large display window was laced in snowflake-shaped lighting that showcased a variety of painted winter landscapes, handmade ornaments, pottery, and other local crafts, along with exquisite cross-stitched pictures, depicting Santa, reindeer, and other Christmas images. As she entered the mellow establishment, Elizabeth was immediately enveloped by the calming ambience of her beloved crafts. She quickly lost herself in the many shelves of stitching designs and the thrilling prospect of finding new projects, which immediately lifted her mood.

As she browsed, she took in the familiar scene of her private refuge and soaked in the multiple scents of homemade candles. There were colorful displays of specialty threads, beads, flosses, designer buttons, Mill Hill and Jim Shore kits, distinctive scissors, project bags, and counting pins in charming figures of animals, birds, fruits, and everything holiday. The walls were tastefully cluttered with framed cross-stitch pieces that the owners and local stitchers had completed, and a table for clearance items, which was always filled with overlooked treasures. Oh, what fun!

In the backroom there was a long, wide table scuffed with use and age, surrounded by a hodgepodge of well worn chairs for anyone wanting to stitch, chat, or learn a new stitching technique. In the corner were two overstuffed blue-printed chintz chairs and a small scarred wooden table for those who just wanted to stop in for a bit of gossip and a hot drink or give a weary back a respite.

"Well, hello, stranger. I didn't see you come in. How have you been?" asked Janice Baker, as she exited the supply room. "I've been so busy I can't keep up with my feet!" she laughed. Janice was in her mid-fifties with curly brown hair. She wore loose-fitting jeans and undistinguished cotton tops all year long. Her large blue spectacles gave her the image of an ancient who was surprised to find anything modern in her existence.

"I know. It's been way too long. It's just been so hectic with the holidays bearing down on us like a feckless teenager driving over the speed limit! How are you, Janice, and where's Cora?"

"Cora's in the back unpacking our new goodies. She just returned from the Great Smoky Mountain Cross-Stitch Convention." Janice brusquely pushed her gargantuan glasses back in place, giving her the appearance of a hoot owl searching for prey.

"Here I am!" Cora called out, emerging from the backroom. "We've missed seeing you. You're going to love these new patterns!" Cora exclaimed, always excited by anything that could be stitched. "Come on in the back, and I'll give you the first look! The stitching companies outdid themselves this year. I had to rope myself in, or I would have spent two budgets in the blink of an eye."

Cora Roberts was a plump and jovial fifty-something-year-old who wore artsy garb, long gaudy earrings, and often dyed her hair in strips of pink or light blue. She was a likable character and passionate about cross stitching. Her dream was to become a full-time designer, and she sold many of her own patterns in the store. Cora was the town's busybody who relished in community gossip. She was known as the go-to girl when anyone sought the inside scoop of village news. Her information was almost always spot on. How did she do it?

Elizabeth lingered for hours, just as she does when browsing for books at the Bibliophile, losing all sense of time. It's as if she is caught in a dreamlike spell, getting lost in the ethereal realm of pages and threads. In the end, she picked up five patterns, a bundle of floss, Aida cloth in a rainbow of colors, and an assortment of Piecemeal needles in various sizes. She even went overboard and bought two sets of counting pins, one Christmas and one featuring beagles.

"Well, you girls were right. This is just what I needed. I can't wait to get home to start. The only problem is which pattern?"

"Start with the one that speaks to you the loudest. That's what I always do," joked Janice. "No one can have too many patterns."

"Don't I know it!" agreed Elizabeth. "You know what? I think I'll take that Nora Corbett sleigh and the three kings by Glendon Place. They're just too beautiful to leave behind!"

"That's my girl!" rallied Janice. " Will you need the fabric and floss for those?"

"Absolutely!" Elizabeth grinned as she gave a hearty thumbs-up.

As Cora rang up her purchases, she leaned forward and whispered conspiratorially, "Did you hear about the robbery last night?"

"Robbery? Goodness, no!" gasped Elizabeth. "How could I have not heard about that? I just came from the Sugar Bowl."

"I think the village is trying to keep it hush-hush, but one of my earlier customers, Martha Cadwallader, said the police lights woke her up late last night, so she went outside to find out what was going on. She said Curtis Hughes was robbed. He's her next-door neighbor, you know, and she's looking to sell that big ole place."

"Wait a minute! Curtis Hughes was robbed last night?" Elizabeth was in disbelief.

"Yes!" Cora exclaimed. "Martha said when Curtis got home from the town meeting, he noticed something was off, so he went to investigate and saw that the dining-room window had been jimmied. He found his mother's jewelry box upside down on the bed and everything in it was gone. Her pearls, diamonds, you name it, all gone! You remember his mother, Nora Hughes? She was very wealthy, and snooty wouldn't begin to describe her."

"Now, Cora," admonished Janice.

"Well, he claims he forgot to set his alarm and called and asked for Officer Ruff. You know Jimmy looks a bit daft, but he's really smart," she continued in a confidential but humorous whisper, hoping Janice wouldn't hear and interrupt again. She should have known better. Janice could hear a fly walking on a leaf a mile away.

Although Officer Jimmy Ruff didn't look and act as though he were playing with a full deck, he had a way of solving puzzles that amazed anyone who knew him well.

Janice, hearing anyway, jumped in and added, "He's got a mind like a steel trap, that man does. He may look like Barney Fife, but he acts just like Sheriff Andy Taylor."

"I can't believe something like this happened in North Falls," said Elizabeth, totally perplexed. Beryl's right, she mused. What is wrong with people today?

"Just think. We've got our own international jewelry thief right here in North Falls. Isn't it exciting!" gushed Cora.

"Now, Cora, don't go overboard. You know how she gets," cautioned Janice, shooting Elizabeth a knowing look.

Once Elizabeth left the shop, her mind was in a flurry. Who, indeed, would do such a thing, and her scarf quickly came to mind...again. She stopped by the Sugar Plum Bakery and purchased a hot herbal tea. As she sipped the soothing liquid, she immediately felt the calming effect and made her way to the village park where she could enjoy the crisp weather, admire the squirrels' antics, and mull over the uncanny events that had plagued her quiet community. As she settled herself in the gazebo, she let her mind wander to the beauty of the upcoming season. She gazed across the park to the line of shops as their owners diligently transformed their small businesses into winter wonderlands. It was just then that a Mercedes pulled into the children's play area, followed by a second familiar jalopy, and then a silver SUV with magnetic placards donning its sides. Three men descended from their vehicles and soon began gesticulating as their angry voices pierced the silence of the early evening.

The raucous shouts felt completely out of place in the tranquil environment. Elizabeth froze so as not to be noticed and strained to see if she recognized any of the three mystery men. The shadows from the flickering streetlamp danced across their faces, distorting their features just enough to keep her guessing. One of them began speaking in a low, calm, and authoritative cadence. Her heart pounded. She knew that voice. She dared not move, afraid even her breath might betray her hiding place.

Is it my imagination, or is that Curtis Hughes, Ollie Williams, and James Powell, the village real estate agent? she conjectured. What in the world would they have to talk about, especially after the way Ollie and Curtis went after each other last night? The men abruptly left, leaving the air charged with vehement intensity. Elizabeth was shaken by the bewildering scene. She remained in the gazebo for quite some time, ruminating on the purpose of such a clandestine meeting, as the temperature dropped and the evening's stillness deepened. Despite the angry eruption and the jewelry theft, something in the night air began to shift. The magic of the season swirled around her, wrapping her in a hush of snow and pine. Then, as if carried on the wind itself, a new thought entered her mind, and with it, an unexpected joy began to bloom. Her daughters would be home soon!

3

Follow-Up to the Big Shindig

orth Falls is a lovely little village that draws tourists each year during the holidays. Many visitors seek a quiet respite before the seasonal rush begins, strolling through quaint shops, sampling sumptuous treats, skating across the glistening lake, or simply curling up with a good book in front of a roaring fire. All of it is made even more magical with a breathtaking view and a steaming cup of hot chocolate in hand.

Now that Christmas was nearing, the shopkeepers were busy embellishing the streets with Christmas cheer, but tonight the park would be filled with community Christmas trees bordering the walkways. Trees were purchased by village members, churches, and businesses from the North Pole Tree Farm, and then individually decorated to outdo their fellow competition. It was a glorious sight to behold as tree after tree lined the paths in a maze of glory, while the Victorian lampposts cast a soft golden glow as evening approached. With the addition of the colorfully lit trees, the park will be metamorphosed into such merry splendor that every visitor will be bewitched with a touch of dreamy holiday enchantment.

As village folks spent the day decorating their individual trees, the official kickoff for Christmas had finally arrived, and preparations for the parade were in full swing. Streets would soon be blocked off as vendors set up their booths, overflowing with holiday wares. Children and parents were lining up for the annual treat bag giveaway to be personally distributed by none other than the honorable Mayor Tom Beeman at the town hall, followed by a visit with Santa, played by Father Christmas himself, Ollie Williams. Tots were jumping up and down in the cold, pulling on the grown-ups' coats in eager anticipation for their yearly pleas to the jolly old elf. Ollie sat on Santa's throne, his red velvet suit gleaming beneath the scintillating lights, with a twinkle in his eye to match.

Ollie lived for this time of year when he could experience the little tykes' Christmas excitement. This truly was the best time of year, he thought. He hoped that each and every one got their hearts' desires, and just to be sure, he contributed a grand donation annually to make sure that all the children in the village had a cheerful holiday. Ollie made his charitable gift anonymously, but most villagers suspected he was the gracious benefactor and loved him even more.

As the last child ambled from the building with treat bag in hand, Ollie gathered up his belongings to get ready for the parade and then relocate to the Holly Hill Inn for the biggest Christmas party of the season. This was an exhausting day for the elder, but he hardly seemed to notice because, just like the children, he loved all the holiday activities the season had to offer, and he refused to miss a single one.

"There you are, Santa," called out Councilman Ellis Lloyd, accompanied by the mayor himself. "Once again, the event was a raging success. I don't know what the children of North Falls would do without you, Santa. Here's a little something extra from the council for our appreciation of having the best dang Santa Claus in the county."

As Ollie was handed an envelope, he raised his hands in protest and said, "Why don't you just keep that and give it to the Children's Christmas Fund?"

"We knew that would be exactly what you would say, so we've already given a separate check in your name to your favorite charity. This is for you, Ollie," the councilman proudly stated.

"Merry Christmas and thanks again," bellowed Mayor Beeman, making sure that all who were lingering nearby could hear his good cheer. He was running for another term next year.

Ah, Christmas was alive and well in North Falls.

***

While the children were lining up for their holiday treats, Elizabeth was browsing in the local grocery, the Welsh Cupboard, and filling her cart with essentials so she wouldn't have to venture out tomorrow. She was so looking forward to the big gala tonight and wanted a quiet day tomorrow to relax and ruminate on the wonderful time she was sure to have at the Holly Hill soiree. Just as Elizabeth was putting the last item on the checkout counter, the dreaded curmudgeon, Mr. Finch, appeared out of nowhere and began bagging her groceries.

Oh, no, thought Elizabeth, just what I need to dampen my spirits. Finch and Elizabeth never seemed to hit it off. He relocated to the village some time ago, after he retired from an obscure past. No one seemed to know where he came from or what he did before showing up in North Falls. In fact, no one even knew his real name. He just went by Finch. Every time Elizabeth visited the Cupboard, he somehow managed to squash her bread, crack an egg or two, or damage some other item. Unfortunately, she never discovered the food vandalism until she unpacked her provisions to be utterly astonished at her findings, yet again. Elizabeth was positive that Finch was adept at hiding the damaged commodities ever so cleverly so she wouldn't discover them until she left the store and, therefore, couldn't make a complaint. Oh, he was good. She could just hear him. "Madam, I am shocked that you would consistently be so clumsy and then attempt to blame me for your incompetence!" What a crusty old geezer!

"So, which of my food items are you planning on sabotaging today? Thank goodness I didn't purchase any eggs or bread."

Finch was busy placing her items into brown paper sacks and didn't respond. Instead, he asked, "Did you hear about the theft? The whole village is talking about nothing else."

"Of course I heard about it. Are you just learning of it? If so, you're about a day late and a dollar short," she replied tersely.

It wasn't like Elizabeth to be snarky, but for some reason, this man got under her skin.

"I heard about it the night it happened, and I must say there is something quite odd about the whole thing," remarked Finch, as he scrunched in way too many items for one sack.

"Why would you say a thing like that? Do you suspect something out of the ordinary?" Elizabeth was so absorbed in his peculiar comment that she was oblivious to his shoddy bagging skills. Her curiosity could get the best of her, especially with so many bizarre events of late.

"Oh, let's just say I have a sixth sense about these things," Finch responded, with a look in his eye Elizabeth wasn't sure she liked.

"Well, I have other errands, so I must be getting on."

"Are you going to the big shindig tonight?" asked the crusty curmudgeon.

"Oh, I'll be there. I don't suppose you'll be attending, will you?"

"Not quite my thing, but I hope you have a good time."

As Elizabeth picked up her groceries and headed to the door, she glanced back, startled to see Crusty watching her go. She started to ask him about that "sixth sense," but just as she opened her mouth, a can of peas escaped from the overloaded bag and rolled under the counter. By the time she retrieved it, the irritant was nowhere to be seen.

There's something not right about that old coot, she thought, as a rogue pear pinwheeled across the pavement. She decided then and there she was going to do some sleuthing herself, for like it or not, there were way too many strange events of late: her stolen Christmas scarf, the volatile town hall meeting, a jewelry theft, the strange meeting in the park, and now...just who was this Finch?

4

The Infamous Christmas Party

The parade was a magical spectacle of lights, whimsical Christmas creatures, vendor sweets, and Ollie as the grand finale, waving from his sleigh and calling out a hearty "Merry Christmas!" as the local high school band filled the air with traditional holiday tunes. The entire village turned out for the event, and now, with cheeks flushed from the cold and hearts full of cheer, many, including Elizabeth and Grace, were making their way home to get ready for the big party on the hill. Elizabeth and Grace would be walking to the inn where they would meet up with Peg and her husband Jack. Beryl and her husband Bill had opted not to attend, as social events were not their niche. They were content just to stay in for the evening.

Bill Thomas was a kind and generous man who had met his wife Beryl at an old-fashioned Halloween party at the North Falls Methodist Church almost sixty years ago. Beryl had come dressed as a hobo, wearing her uncle's oversized overalls and carrying a kerchief tied to a stick. Her face was smeared with ashes from the fireplace, and she was certain no one would guess her identity. She had just finished bobbing for apples when she noticed a group of boys from Mapleville who had crashed the party. Among them was Bill, watching her with keen interest.

When she left for home later that night, Bill was so smitten he took a chance and followed her. As she crossed the white picket fence, he called out. Surprised, she turned to find him standing there, grinning in the moonlight.

Without thinking, Bill leaned over the fence in a bold attempt to kiss her. That brazen act earned him a swift and stinging smack across his cheek.

"Good girls don't kiss on the first date!" Beryl snapped, quoting one of her mother's old Morgan family rules.

Although he didn't get his kiss that night, he did eventually steal her heart and was rewarded with fifty-six years of marital bliss.

Bill would watch television tonight as Beryl read the paper, catching up on the events of the day. There, in their cozy home, they would remain happy as clams as the townsfolk hobnobbed with the socially elite, dancing and drinking as the night wore on.

Grace and Elizabeth paired up for the night since both were single ladies, and then the foursome would stroll through the park on their way home to admire the display of lighted trees and welcome in the Yuletide.

Elizabeth had taken her beagle Abner for a walk earlier, noticing the drop in temperature. Once they reached home, she gave her small companion plenty of doting attention and a much loved treat. Oh, how she loved that dog!

It was quite a touching story as to how Elizabeth and Abner found each other. She had gone into Mapleville, located in the next county, to pick up a prescription and do some serious grocery shopping due to the limited variety (and bagging skills) at the Cupboard.

Standing near the in-store cafe, were a stick thin and sickly pale middle-aged couple. Their clothing hung on them like Little Lost John, barely concealing the raw, angry scabs peeking from the frayed cuffs of their winter coats. Their eyes were glassy and red rimmed, exposing a life of hard living. In their shopping cart, of all places, was a tri-colored puppy. Elizabeth, unable to resist, charged toward the puppy like a moth to a flame. Approaching the cart, the puppy perked up, excitedly wagging its tail a million miles a minute. "Excuse me," she asked politely. "Can I pet your puppy?" As the small canine licked her fingers hungrily, Elizabeth felt a magnetic pull.

"We'll sell him to ya for a hundred dollars. He's a purebred beagle." The gaunt man spoke fast, like a practiced salesman, desperately trying to make a sale.

"If you don't take him, we're goin' have to put him down," added the haggard woman, hastily.

"Oh, no, don't do that!" exclaimed Elizabeth. She suddenly felt a soul-stirring revelation, intuitively knowing there was no way she could walk away.

Interrupting her thoughts, the man quickly responded, "We'll give him to you for *fifty* dollars."

Perplexed and undecided about what to do in this unusual situation, Elizabeth took one last look at the pup's pleading eyes, instantly realizing this was her dog. She responded, "I'll tell you what. I'll buy your groceries if you give me the pup."

The man didn't hesitate. "Deal! But can you throw in a gallon of ice cream?"

"And a carton of soda?" added his mate, her eyes flickering with excited anticipation of a rare indulgence.

After a heart-to-heart conversation, kindhearted Elizabeth bought the couple groceries in exchange for her new addition, innately knowing that he was the best bargain she would ever make at any grocery store.

Once in the car, Elizabeth held the tiny canine so they could look one another eye-to-eye and said, "I'm going to call you Little Abner, just like the the character in the comic strip when I was a kid. It's the perfect name for you." She set him in her lap where he stayed, quite contented, until they reached North Falls. That beagle pup stole Elizabeth's heart that day and gave salve to her wounded spirit. They were true soulmates, and the way Abner was placed in her path, Elizabeth had no doubt that the Universe had sent her this very special gift to help her through a difficult time.

"Bye, my sweet boy," babbled Elizabeth. As she made the necessary preparations to exit her home to attend the gala, she felt an uneasy premonition. It quickly dissipated as she was filled with eager anticipation for her twins' homecoming and, of course, all the delicacies that awaited.

***

The Holly Hill Inn was a grand old establishment of Colonial brick perched upon a hillock on the outskirts of town. A long paved driveway circled the front lawn where an elaborate fountain spun delicate patterns across a small pool, enhanced with underwater red and green lighting. The twenty-foot white pillars framed an entrance of tall, wide, dark-wooden double doors with oversized brass knobs. Gigantic pine wreaths hung on each door, adorned with candied fruit, colorful lights, massive bulbs in every hue, and bright red ribbons. The inn and its surrounding grounds were known for flamboyant decorations, but this year it proved to be a sight to behold. The new proprietors, Ed and Virginia Pierce, had gone up and beyond to outdo the former owners, and everyone in the village couldn't wait to see the final results.

No one really knew much information about the Pierces, who arrived shortly after the North Falls Community Church minister took the pulpit. The "out-of-towners," as the community referred to the Pierces, just popped up suddenly when the Nelsons, the original owners of the Holly Hill Inn, retired, moved to Florida, and sold the well respected hotel and restaurant.

This evening Elizabeth wore an emerald green pantsuit, accented by a dazzling diamond broach in the shape of a massive snowflake, pinned on her lapel. Matching emerald earrings, ring, bracelet, and necklace were graced with diamonds. She was, without a doubt, a vision of winter elegance.

Her mid-length black mink coat was paired with a matching muff, embellished with an identical snowflake to the broach she wore. It was a subtle nod to the season she loved. All the adornments were thoughtful and expensive gifts from her daughters, who loved to spend lavishly on their mother. Elizabeth stopped to pick up Grace, and they walked the short distance to the party.

Grace was adorned in a modest black pantsuit that suited her regal demeanor. Her lovely gold-trimmed jacket fitted her perfectly. A black fox stole rested gracefully across her shoulders, adding a timeless appeal to her already flawless appearance. She and Elizabeth were not just sisters, but dear friends, and tonight, wrapped in the excitement of the season, they felt blessed to spend the evening together.

"You know, when Peg and Jack were younger, they used to go dancing all the time. They were a stunning couple. Why, when they walked into a room, every eye turned to them." Grace secretly yearned for a romance like Peg and Jack. She loved to reminisce about stories from her youth and would tell Elizabeth, her much younger sister, these tales over and over.

Although Grace, Beryl, and Peg were much older than their baby sister, they always welcomed Elizabeth into their inner circle as an equal. They were a tight-knit group and entertaining "as all get out." Everyone enjoyed their company.

As the sisters neared the inn's property, they were mesmerized with what was before them. "Wow, look at that! Breathtaking," exhaled Grace, and it was. Christmas trees bedecked in colorful lights were scattered masterfully about the grounds to enhance the Christmas theme, as garland, white twinkling lights, red bows, and gold garnishments completed the ensemble. Snowflakes began to fall, sprinkling the holiday scene as if on cue from a Hallmark movie.

"Oh, it's more than perfect!" exclaimed Elizabeth. "I can't wait to see what the Pierces have done with the interior."

"Tell me about the new proprietors," urged Grace.

"Well, all I've heard about them is their first names, Ed and Virginia, and they are quite aloof and, well, standoffish. Odd characteristics for folks taking over a business in a new town, don't you think? Perhaps I'll stop by the stitch shop and have a chat with Cora. If anyone would know, it would be Cora."

"Perhaps they're just private folks."

"No one is just 'private folks' in this village. I'll make sure we get introduced tonight. I'd love to tell them how splendid everything looks," Elizabeth said with a smile, letting her gaze drift over the scene. She took a breath, tucking it all away like a keepsake to remember. The Pierces had definitely outdone the previous owners.

***

"They certainly deserve recognition for this extravaganza," piped Grace as they entered the inn. "It's just stunning!"

The party was in full swing, overflowing with tantalizing food, contagious laughter, and infectious excitement. Guests sipped on the signature festive cocktail, the Sleigh Ride, while dancing to lively holiday tunes. Amid the merriment, a sense of anticipation filled the air. Unbeknownst to them, a mystery guest was already among them. Marshall Wymark, a supposedly up-and-coming author of horror fiction, seemed to have had one too many Sleigh Rides. Since no one in North Falls would read such an appalling genre, no one recognized him as the celebrity he believed himself to be. "He must be a friend of the Pierces," whispered Peg. "I've never seen him before."

As the night wound down, Peg finally took a break from dancing with her dashing mate Jack as he headed for the (spiked) punch table. She wore a long silver dress that shimmered with every step, and her matching shoes looked as if they were chosen for twirling, not standing. Peg never demanded attention, but somehow it always found her. Never far from her side, Jack was the epitome of holiday charm in an impeccable gray suit, crisp white shirt, and a bright red tie cheerfully printed with sprigs of holly. Together they made quite the debonair couple.

"He's really not bad looking," said Grace, as the conversation reverted back to the author's mysterious presence. Grace had been married once, but it had ended badly. She discovered, quite by accident, that her ex had been unfaithful with one of her friends. She promptly gathered all Peter's belongings and left them on the front porch to welcome him when he returned, along with freshly installed bright new shiny locks. Grace is not one to dally when major decisions need to be made and refuses to wallow in self pity over her former husband's unscrupulous actions.

Peg took a big swig of her Sleigh Ride and giggled her approval of Grace's assessment with a mischievous wink.

"He's got an attitude. I can smell it all the way over here," chuffed Elizabeth. "I don't like men who think they're good looking. Can't be trusted."

"He keeps looking over here," whispered Peg conspiratorially. "Oh, he's headed this way!"

The alleged horror writer, who had been eyeing the sisters all evening, sashayed across the room like a graceful swan. He was, in fact, a very handsome man with thick silver hair, piercing dark eyes, and an aquiline nose that made him look like an exotic Mediterranean. He was dressed in a black suit which had to be expensive because it fit him like a glove, a very costly glove; his dress shirt was an interesting hue of deep mint green, with a matching variegated tie and handkerchief, expertly positioned in his jacket pocket. This man knew how to dress.

"Hello, ladies. I'm Marshall Wymark. It's nice to see you're enjoying yourselves."

"Of course we are," said Elizabeth, with a slight edge of annoyance she couldn't quite hide. "It's a Christmas party. Who doesn't love a holiday bash?"

"So true. I was wondering if you may do me the honor of a waltz, charming lady?" requested Marshall zealously, as he took Grace in from head to toe.

"Oh, I haven't danced in ages. I'm much too rusty," Grace replied warily.

"Well, let's give it a try, shall we?" Marshall responded coquettishly, and off they glided.

"Oh, I didn't know Grace knew how to dance like that," said Elizabeth, taken aback with the scene unfolding before her.

"Oh, yes. In our day, we were quite the dancers," murmured Peg. "Excuse me, Elizabeth, but I need another spin on the floor before these old feet give out. Where's Jack?" With that, she was off, in search of her husband and grabbing another Sleigh Ride on the way.

If one thought the outdoor decorations were lavish, the indoor embellishments were over the top. Greenery laced with twinkling white lights, gold glittery bulbs, and red velvet ribbons graced every mantle, stairway, and threshold. Elegant Santas, reindeer, icicles, gorgeously wrapped presents, and everything Christmas was placed with perfection. The whole inn radiated warmth, with a glamorous, yet cozy feel. It was truly a magical evening, and the Sleigh Ride was undoubtedly a holiday hit.

"So, what brings you to our little village? Do you have family here?" inquired Grace as they floated ever so gracefully across the dance floor.

"Oh no, dear lady. I was actually invited by..." but his reply was interrupted by a loud crash and raised voices. Curtis Hughes and James Powell were glaring at each other over a tray of broken champagne glasses. The fruity liquid was pooling onto the marble floor. Although it was obvious the two were quite angry, they had the good sense to call a truce. Curtis abruptly exited to the adjoining room as James took off for who knows where, and the partygoers, dressed in their evening finery, acted as if nothing were amiss as one of the many hosting staff quickly soaked up the spill. Virginia Pierce, chatting quietly with the new community pastor, John White, was quick to react by asking everyone to greet another surprise guest. As the band began to play "Santa Claus Is Coming to Town," entering as if right on cue, Ollie, still in his Santa garb with his merry demeanor and huge holiday smile, burst through the threshold with a jolly, "Ho, ho, ho! Merry Christmas!" Everyone clapped and cheered as he made his way around the vast room, distributing chocolates and other confectionery treats. He mischievously asked the guests what they wanted most for Christmas, secretly promising to pass their wishes to their spouses for a heads up on the perfect gift. Ollie has an excellent memory, and as everyone knows everyone, he danced about delivering the momentous information. The angry spectacle was soon forgotten, as the jaunty atmosphere quickly returned.

***

As the three sisters and Jack set out after an exhilarating evening, they discussed the events of the night as the snow continued to accumulate, making walking a bit treacherous.

"So what was going on with you and the handsome stranger? Marshall Wymark, wasn't it? I'm itching to find out," Peg said with a devious smile, nudging her younger sister and slipping on the walkway. "He was quite smitten with you, Grace, and I think the feeling was mutual."

"Oh, he was quite the charmer," Grace admitted, as she reminisced about the very pleasant dance, and, if she were honest, the attention the attractive and personable author gave her. Grace may be a septuagenarian, but she wasn't over-the-hill yet, at least not in her mind's eye.

"You're not going to see him again, are you?" asked Elizabeth, not too happy that a possible relationship could be brewing with, in her opinion, an unsavory character that no one knew the first thing about.

"Well, he did ask if I'd like to have dinner at the inn. I do love the prime rib, and I'm actually looking forward to it."

"Did he say whom he was staying with, or how long he's in town, or why he's here of all places?" interrogated Elizabeth as she continued peppering her sibling with questions and acting like a carbon copy of Beryl.

"No, Elizabeth, he didn't specify for how long he would be here, or whom he was staying with, or why he was even here in the first place." Grace humorously mimicked her sister, repeating her questions with exaggerated exasperation. "In fact, now that I think about it, he didn't say much about himself at all. But he sure wanted to know all he could about me, including whether I was attached," tittered Grace, and then ever so softly, as if to herself, "It was such a fun evening."

"Did anyone get to talk with either of the Pierces? I didn't get the chance. The night got away from me. It was such a grand kickoff to Christmas," slurred Peg. "One of the best."

"I agree. I haven't danced like that in quite some time. And the punch was delicious!" declared Jack.

"Oh, Jack, you should know. You practically drank the whole bowl!" sniggered Peg.

"Actually, I did," chuckled Jack in the cutest giggle ever. As soon as he recovered, he added, "And I did get the chance to speak with Ed, but he was quite distant. I couldn't get the first thing out of him. It was as if he were purposely being evasive," ruminated Jack. "In fact, I would even go as far as to say he was dodging my questions pretty skillfully."

"I think that's odd. How are you going to get to know people if you don't open up a little?" added Grace.

"I think they're hiding something," hiccuped Peg.

"It was as if Pierce were a professional at diverting direct answers, along with Wymark. In fact, it seems to me they were both evading information, which is really odd," acknowledged Jack, who thought he had contributed an excellent point to the conversation and was quite pleased with his observations.

"I tried to speak with Virginia at the dessert table, but she looked as if she had seen a ghost and couldn't get out of Dodge fast enough. It was somewhat uncomfortable," admitted Elizabeth.

It's because you're an English teacher, and you dress like a forty-foot millionaire," Peg reasoned. "No, I'm serious, Elizabeth. You intimidate a lot of people."

I wished I intimidated sourpuss Finch. That man gets on my last nerve! Elizabeth thought to herself. "Honestly, I can't help it. It's the teacher in me. I'm always wanting people to speak correctly. If they only knew how close we were to losing our language. Why, in 1066..."

"We know. The French took the crown. Moving on," prompted Peg, not wanting to hear a repeated lecture on the history of the English language.

"Let's see if we can perhaps befriend them," suggested Grace. "It must be so difficult relocating with no family or friends nearby. Let's invite Virginia to lunch at the Sugar Bowl! Beryl is always the best hostess."

The snow continued to mount, turning the park into a Christmas scene worthy of any exorbitant holiday card. "Oh, look at the colors!" exclaimed Elizabeth, who was as thrilled at the sight of the vibrant exhibition as any child. "Let's go for a stroll through the trees! It's almost Christmas!" And off went the jovial pack, giggling and delighting in the magnificent time they all had shared.

The brightly lit parade of festive conifers was stunning as the revelers meandered along the illuminated path. Just beyond, Grace caught sight of a strange feature disrupting the pristine blanket of snow. She stopped in her tracks. "What is that?" she asked, her breath fogging in the cold night air, as she pointed toward the distorted silhouette.

Their laughter tapered off as the rhythm of their steps faltered. The entourage then fell silent as they stood peering into the darkness. They began to move as one toward the strange mass that did not appear to be part of the cheery scene.

There in the mounting snow, lay a not-so-jolly elf with a scarf that screamed, "I'm expensive" and "Christmas is here!" wound tightly around his throat. "Hells bells," said Peg. "Someone's killed Santa Claus!"

5

A Perplexing Meeting

As everyone expected, Officer Jimmy Ruff was extremely interested in discovering how Elizabeth's scarf showed up as the murder weapon. His questioning was extensive and thorough, but Elizabeth, like the others, had no answers. Each offered a list of reliable witnesses who would give them substantial alibis, and after several tense hours, Elizabeth and her entourage were released and made it home, around two in the morning. Naturally, everyone assumed the corpse was Ollie. After all, he'd been the life of the gala, striding through the ballroom in his Father Christmas robes and booming with laughter. But then came the real shock (and relief). It wasn't the beloved old elf, but the suave mystery guest and Grace's possible new beau, Marshall Wymark, the author everyone had whispered about all evening!

"Grace, I'm so sorry about Mr. Wymark. You two seemed to really hit it off," Peg said softly, her voice barely rising above the sound of their heels, slipping on the hazardous walkway. She gently threaded her arm through Grace's, a simple gesture of comfort as they trudged through the mounting snow. Each was eager to reach the warmth of home after the terrible discovery of Wymark, lying beneath the falling snow, not unlike a character from one of his own novels.

Grace swallowed hard and leaned into Peg's shoulder. "Yes, it was quite fun to be courted in that way again and quite shocking to dance with someone and then find him dead." And drat, she thought, he was so good looking.

But the real question was how did Elizabeth's stolen scarf end up as the murder weapon.

As the group dissipated into the night from the drab, smelly police station, Elizabeth, Peg, and Grace agreed to meet at the Bibliophile later that day. Peg would alert Beryl to the alarming news and the scheduled meeting at the bookshop. Before they all headed for their homes, there were plenty of hugs and comforting reassurances. They fervently vowed they would discover how Elizabeth's scarf was used as the murder weapon; thus, the Morgan Sisters Sleuthing Club was born.

Elizabeth thanked them all as she made her way home alone, but she was pondering if the use of her scarf was somehow blatantly pointing the blame at her, and, if so, why?

Something in the quaint village was definitely askew with the internal conflicts involving the proposed expansion, the uncanny bickering, Curtis's break-in and theft, the odd meeting in the park, and now a murder! Oh, yes, something was not right in the beautiful and quaint Snowflake Village. But for the life of Elizabeth and her siblings, no one had a clue.

***

The Bibliophile was located across the street from Grace's antique store. As Elizabeth entered the bookshop at two o'clock sharp, she was once again swept away by the conventional charm of polished wooden shelves, the smell of beeswax, immaculately displayed holiday embellishments, colorful novelty ornaments, and the aroma of tantalizing baked treats and freshly brewed tea. Ah, she could almost feel the tension melting. But then...she stopped dead in her tracks.

Before her sat five individuals: three were her beloved siblings, one she did not recognize, and the other she wished she didn't. The first individual was a young woman drenched in black who had tattoos strung along her arms, and, in Elizabeth's opinion, some obviously misplaced piercings. Miss Goth's short, dark hair was cut in a jagged style with subtle midnight-blue highlights that actually suited her well. The youngest guest was so oddly out of sorts that it was obvious she was excruciatingly uncomfortable.

The other member was an older gentleman with a full head of white hair, worn a little long, and intense blue eyes that twinkled mischievously as if he were the only one in the room clever enough to catch an intellectual joke. His face was undeniably handsome, but his demeanor exuded a quiet arrogance, the kind that spoke, "I'm smarter than you, and I know it." He wore pressed khakis and a crisply starched white button-down, brown loafers, and a navy jacket which gave him the appearance of someone headed for his first day of prep school.

Elizabeth took one look at him and exclaimed, "What are you doing here?"

"I heard about your clandestine powwow and felt I could be of some assistance, so…here I am," answered Finch as he spread his arms wide as if to say, "This is my gift to you."

"Well, you have quite the nerve," retorted Elizabeth.

"Actually, it's my fault," blurted Peg, making a moot attempt at breaking the mounting tension. "I just kind of hinted at a secret get-together at the bookshop..."

"...and we took Finch up on his invitation. We believe him to be useful in our, shall we say, investigation," piped in Grace, excited at the thought of having two crimes committed right under their noses.

"Why in the name of Thor would you think that?" Elizabeth said rather emphatically as she looked each sister in the eye for the need of a feasible explanation. The sisters were all on edge. It was no secret Elizabeth's dislike for the "ole sourpuss."

"Well," stammered Grace and then more quickly, "it was Beryl's idea," obviously throwing the ball into her sister's court.

"Beryl? I'm totally confused. Would someone please explain?" asked Elizabeth, thoroughly disgusted that the private meeting had turned into a community event.

"It's really quite simple," Beryl answered. "Finch and I have become rather good friends. He's been so good to save me the freshest vegetables as soon as they're delivered, so when he heard of the murder, we got to chatting at the Cupboard, and he explained he could be a useful asset, and I quite agreed, so... here he is." Whew, thought Beryl, that was quite a mouthful!

"An asset?" Elizabeth couldn't believe her ears.

"We're getting ahead of ourselves," interjected Finch, way too self-assuredly for Elizabeth's taste.

Why, he thinks he's going to take over, mused Elizabeth. Over my dead body. Oops! Wrong choice of words. She then turned to the group and asked, "And who's she?"

"This is Ana Rees, my new employee," informed Beryl.

"Your new employee? I've never seen her before." Elizabeth was totally baffled at the turn of events and none too happy.

"Well, actually, you may have seen her but just didn't notice her. Ana's first day was the day you reported your Christmas scarf was stolen. I'm sure you were too upset to have heeded her," Beryl stated breathlessly as she turned to Ana. "Please explain why I have included you in our murder mystery case."

"Hold on," interrupted Elizabeth. "Are you related to *Owen* Rees?"

Looking as if she would rather blend in with the wallpaper than answer the question, Ana squeaked, "Yes. He's my father."

Elizabeth remembered Owen, none too fondly, from her teaching days. His middle name was Trouble.

"And you're here because...?"

"I am very good at...well... computers." Ana's voice dropped in volume as did her confidence. `

"Yes, but tell her about what you just told me," urged Beryl.

"If I may interrupt," said Finch, "there is so much more to this than meets the eye, so let's start with what we know."

"Yes, please do, *Mr.* Finch," Elizabeth responded, a bit snarky, which turned the tension up a notch. Mr. Finch appeared not to notice her sarcasm and continued.

"Why don't you sit down and get comfortable? I know this is a lot to take in," cooed Peg, as she handed Elizabeth a cup of cinnamon and clove tea.

Elizabeth tried to calm herself with the rich aroma of the tea, but it didn't quell the irritation she felt bubbling inside. The meeting was arranged for her benefit, but somewhere along the line, the train jumped the track. Who were these people invading her private meeting, and why were the invitations to the girl and the nuisance extended without her knowledge?

"There is more going on here than meets the eye," repeated Finch.

"Yes, so you have previously stated," replied Elizabeth, as she blew out a breath of frustration.

"For instance," completely unfazed by Elizabeth's second interruption, "the town hall meeting is ground zero, in my opinion."

"And why is that?" cut in Elizabeth, refusing to lose control of her meeting.

"Because that is where an altercation occurred between Curtis Hughes and Ollie Williams and the theft of your Christmas scarf. Didn't it seem a bit odd to any of you the level of vehemence of those gentlemen's confrontation? It was totally out of character for both of them," he proclaimed in an aristocratic tone.

"It was absolutely embarrassing the way those two acted. I was shocked, especially at Ollie's behavior," chimed in Beryl.

"For goodness' sake, yes, he's Santa Claus!" clarified Peg.

"Then there is the overheated exchange between Ollie Williams, Curtis Hughes, and James Powell in the park that you witnessed, Elizabeth."

"And how do you know about that? The only person I told was...Beryl?"

"Beryl told me about it and said I should tell Finch," said Grace quickly, pointing at Beryl to let herself off the hook, again.

"And then there are the questions of who stole your scarf and how it became the murder weapon, and most importantly, who dressed our victim, Mr. Wymark, in the Santa costume and why? That's outrageous," concluded Finch.

As thoughts were twirling about in Elizabeth's mind, another very important thought came to her concerning the pest.

"Excuse me, but if Ana is the computer girl, which I am still not sure what that's all about, what credentials do you have to interrupt our 'clandestine powwow'?" inquired Elizabeth, as she emphatically made air quotes.

Finch was quite the enigma in the sleepy village of North Falls. One day, he isn't here, and the next, he is positioned at the Cupboard as the inept, cantankerous bag boy. He appeared out of nowhere, and not one single person in all the county knows the first thing about him. He is the definition of a mystery man. Elizabeth and her gang often spoke of Finch's mysterious past and came to their own conclusions.

Grace thought he was a widower and came to escape troubling memories of a lost love.

Peg thought he was in the witness protection program for a deadly deed, obviously tied to the Mafia, and turned state's evidence.

Beryl surmised he was from the TV show, The Boss, discreetly filming to see how smoothly the Cupboard was running and would surprise one of his employees with a generous financial gift. She was secretly hoping they all might make an appearance on her favorite reality show.

Elizabeth, however, never really voiced her opinion as to where the grocery saboteur came from. Her thoughts seemed to center on a grouchy senior citizen whose family threw him out because he got on their last nerve as he did hers.

"Well, I would like you all to give me your word that what I am about to tell you must never be repeated. It must remain confidential."

Oh dear, he's married, Grace inwardly groaned. She hated being wrong.

Ah ha! thought Peg. He is in the witness protection program. Peg loved being right.

Yes! thought Beryl, he is the Welsh Cupboard's big cheese, and he doesn't want us to ruin the TV show.

Just what I thought, a crusty old geyser whose family kicked him to the curb and, no doubt, probably a criminal on the run to boot, mused Elizabeth.

"I'm a former federal judge," began Finch, as all faces fell and mouths gaped open, "and I have sat over some pretty high-profile cases, so I looked for a quiet little out-of-the-way village to retire in peace with no journalists (or hardened criminals) to pester me in my golden years. That's why it's imperative for you to keep my little secret under wraps. Do I have your word?"

"Absolutely!" said Grace, flabbergasted.

"We've got your back! You can trust us!" echoed Peg.

"You've got my word," said Beryl quite seriously.

"What about you?" Finch turned and looked directly at Elizabeth.

"Oh, do you doubt my honesty?" exaggerated Elizabeth, as though her word was in question.

"Not in the least, my lady."

Elizabeth started to say I'm not your lady, but held her tongue, which she was not known to do often. "Thank you. Mums the word," and zipped her mouth rather dramatically.

"Ana?"

"Absolutely, Judge Finch." Realizing her breach, Ana's neck and cheeks turned crimson, and she quickly corrected herself. "I mean, Mr. Finch."

"I appreciate your discretion more than you know," confessed Finch, relieved to share a bit of his past with new friends whom he felt sure he could trust.

As everyone held their collective breath, Grace was the first to recover. "Well, I must say, that's impressive."

"You mean you're not the corporate owner of the Welsh Cupboard?" Beryl stated in disbelief and clearly disappointed that she would not be making a TV appearance.

"Where in the world did you get that idea?" He laughed. "That's mighty creative, Beryl!"

"Much better than mine. I was sure you were a criminal on the run," smirked Elizabeth.

"Ha, I'm sure you did," Finch said, curling his lip in amusement, clearly savoring her sharp-witted banter.

"I kind of thought the same. Witness protection," giggled Peg, as she smacked her thigh in mirth.

"Did you have an idea, Grace?" pumped Finch gently, eager to know what the noble pillar of North Falls had thought.

"Oh." The question was so pointed, it caught her off guard. Dare I say it? she wondered. Will he think I'm interested? Which I definitely am not. I don't want to hurt his feelings. At least my idea isn't as blatant as Elizabeth's, but still I can't lie. She took a breath and commenced tentatively. "I thought perhaps you were a widower in need of a change of scenery," and then quickly added, "but I don't think you're here for any nefarious reasons."

"You mean like finding a new mate, like that would ever happen," added Elizabeth, under her breath.

Finch did, in fact, overhear Elizabeth but elected to ignore yet another dig from the plucky retired educator.

"What about you, Ana? Any ideas?" Finch asked.

Ana shrugged her shoulders as though she had never thought about it, but Ana knew exactly who Finch was before he ever revealed the truth of his past profession, thus the Freudian slip earlier.

"So," asked Elizabeth, "what is your real name, since we all agreed to keep your little secret?"

"Magnus Finch, dear lady, at your service. Magnus means 'great one' in Latin."

"And Finch means 'to swindle,'" she smiled wickedly. "I hope you will think twice before doing anything like that, although, I must say, I personally wouldn't put it past you," smirked Elizabeth, happily surmising she got the last jab.

"Oh, my beautiful lady, I would never think of swindling you," uttered Finch unctuously, then he winked at Elizabeth with those big baby blues, and she did something she rarely ever does...she blushed.

***

An hour later, the meeting adjourned with no more drama; however, the tension was still wafting about the room like a paper airplane. The newly formed detective group discussed all the uncanny events, and Judge Magnus Finch took extensive notes, promising to put everything down in an orderly, noteworthy fashion to be distributed at their next meeting on Wednesday at six o'clock to accommodate everyone's schedule. Elizabeth took special notice of Finch's itinerary and decided to visit the Cupboard on his day off to avoid him at all costs.

It seemed inevitable, according to the judge, that this was only the beginning of something much more sinister than any of them realized. He pompously stated that he was absolutely certain another incident was imminent. "I've seen this kind of scenario many times before," he stated pedantically.

"Of course you have," Elizabeth snorted under her breath, as she thought, My dear, beautiful lady. Hogwash!

***

As the friends meandered toward their respective destinations, Grace and Elizabeth walked together to discuss the meeting's outcome further. "I don't know why, but that man gets under my skin quicker than a flea in a dog pound," confessed Elizabeth.

"Yes, I think everyone would agree on that, but why exactly is that, Elizabeth?" asked Grace, as she tried to conceal an ear-splitting grin.

"He's just so arrogant and smug about every little thing." Elizabeth began to mock him, surprisingly quite accurately, as she shook her head, lowered her voice, and pulled her shoulders back. " 'I've seen this kind of scenario many times before.' I don't mean to be unkind, but honestly, does he have to sound like he's narrating a documentary about how right he always is?"

"Well, I do trust his past experience. He obviously saw quite a bit in the federal court system. I bet he could write one scary book on what he's seen and heard. And when he said he predicted there were to be more strange and sinister occurrences, it really made me queasy. If he's right, I wonder what we can expect next?" reflected Grace, as she put her wooly mittens on to combat the cold.

"Oh, he's just bloviating. I don't think we will ever see anything else explode like a theft and a murder. I mean, there is only so much that can happen in a sleepy little town like ours. We won't see anything like this again in a million years," Elizabeth postulated.

Oh, if she only knew how wrong she was.

6

The Reveal

Everyone arrived just before six on Wednesday, including the goth girl, still in black garb, minus the matching lipstick. Finch was strutting about like cock robin as though he had something pertinent to divulge, as everyone took a seat, waiting to receive a treat from the Bibliophile's cafe. Entered Peg, right on cue, carrying steaming mugs of raspberry-lemon tea that smelled heavenly. She returned once again from the kitchen, pushing an adorable tiny cart adorned with a basket of scones of the same fruity ingredients, creamy butter, delicate china dessert plates with a variety of Christmas scenes, and the appropriate silverware. It was so tantalizing that Elizabeth thought Finch's head would blow off. If only!

After everyone had retrieved their tasty tidbits and gotten comfortable, Finch started immediately with his plan. Everyone listened intently, including Elizabeth, for he was meticulous in his forthcoming information.

"We need to address exactly who this Marshall Wymark was. He showed up unexpectedly in our little community, made one appearance, and was immediately murdered in, of all things, a Santa suit. Why was he killed, and why the Santa garb?" The Santa suit was the puzzle piece Finch just couldn't wrap his head around, and it was driving him mad.

"It wasn't just the absurdity of it," he emphasized. "It was the deliberateness." He let that sink in before continuing. "I've seen plenty of chaos in my time, but this wasn't chaos. This was calculated. Someone wanted Marshall Wymark dead, and they wanted it done in a way the whole town wouldn't forget. A man murdered is one thing, but a man murdered in a Santa suit? That's theater."

The sleuthing club sat in stunned silence as Finch's assessment took hold. They exchanged glances, the weight of the truth settling heavily over them. In that moment, a unanimous decision was made. They would accept the responsibility and the risks of unmasking whoever had pulled them into this twisted game. Mission Christmas Scarf was on!

After several seconds, Beryl broke in, hoping to give a spark of light to the dark scenario. "This is exactly why I brought Ana in. Ana, please explain your unusual talent."

Ana went from pale to a sickly pallor. Elizabeth thought for sure the young goth girl might faint dead away on the spot. What in the world is going on with this girl? thought Elizabeth. Ana remained frozen.

"Is it because Finch is here? Why, he isn't going to put you in jail. I promise. Go on, tell them," Beryl gently urged.

"What is it, Ana? I'm not going to prosecute you, even if I could, which I can't. Everything said in our meetings stays confidential. If we are to catch this killer and discover whatever else is going on, we must trust each other," beseeched Finch. "Now, please continue."

Ana looked at each member, lingering just a tad longer on Elizabeth. "I'm good at computers," she stated just above a whisper.

"Oh, it's more than that. A lot more. Go on, dear," Beryl said encouragingly.

"I am..."

"You're a what?" Peg said, barely holding back from the suspense.

"She's a hack," confirmed Beryl.

"Goodness," said Grace.

"And she's very good, as we all shall see," Beryl proudly stated.

"A hack? I don't get it. Why would you need a computer hacker?" questioned Elizabeth.

"Oh, I don't need one, until now that is," grinned Beryl.

"Young lady," began Finch.

"Her name's Ana," Beryl gently reminded him.

"Ana," began Finch again, "please relax and understand no one is going to harm you or put you in jail for your acquired skills. Now, please explain."

Why, the old geyser has a bit of compassion! Who would have thought the crusty old beast had it in him? thought Elizabeth. At that point, she felt a motherly tendency to protect Miss Goth.

"Please, Ana. We need to understand what's going on," Elizabeth gently prodded, as she made eye contact with the spindly individual.

Ana dropped her eyes and clenched her hands so tightly her knuckles turned white. "I have always had a thing for computers since I was a kid. It's like all I wanted to do. We didn't have much, but a nice neighbor gave me his broken up old PC, and I tore into it. I figured stuff out, learned shortcuts, messed with

videos for fun, and then I eventually... learned how to hack."
Her voice dropped as she continued.

"I used it on the mean girls, the ones who spread rumors and
wrote horrible stuff about kids like me who aren't part of their
'little club.' I read their messages.

When the bullying wouldn't stop, I started sending anony-
mous warnings and threatened to expose them if they didn't
quit. I flipped the script. I can't stand bullies. People have judged
me my whole life for things my dad and his family did. Stuff I
had nothing to do with." Ana instantly regretted saying anything. It seemed the air between the elderly group and her had
become heavy with the things she hadn't meant to say. She clung
tighter to her hands, wishing she could take the words back.
Why had she said all that? Her chest tightened and her pulse
began to race. She expelled a shaky breath as the suffocating
silence screamed in her head. Her eyes dropped to the floor once
again, afraid of seeing disapproving looks upon their faces. It
was all too much for her. She wished a hole would open up and
swallow her whole.

Breaking the silence, Elizabeth said, "I can't stand bullies either." She had seen enough of it during her teaching career, and
nothing made her angrier.

Elizabeth felt a jolt of guilt. She realized, with a start, that she had been guilty of prejudging Ana because of her father's stunts. She silently chastised herself. Her heart went out to the impressive young woman sitting before her, still anxiously wringing her hands. Elizabeth was determined to make amends.

"Those girls made my life and others miserable because we weren't as pretty or as popular, or as rich. I'm not sorry for what I did." Ana sat back, crossing her arms tightly across her chest like a shield and clenching her jaw until it ached. She braced herself for the lecture or reprimand she was sure to receive for her unorthodox antics.

"Did your 'flipping the script' work?" asked Elizabeth gingerly.

"It drove them nuts. Scared them too." Ana said, her voice trembling but sharper now. She finally loosened her grip, her hands still shaking as she fiddled with the sleeves of her hoodie. "I just wanted them to feel the same kind of fear they were making kids like me feel, you know? To just stop. So...yeah. It worked."

"Good for you, girl," commended Grace, feeling very proud of Ana's honest fortitude.

"Hells bells. That's quite the story," commented Peg, who looked as forlorn as everyone felt. "Thank goodness we girls never experienced anything like that growing up. It's despicable, just despicable."

My, the world is a different place, thought Finch, who was so used to the criminal mind and the horrific things people did to one another. He suddenly felt very protective of this young girl.

"So, how are you proposing to help us with this case?" asked Finch. "And if I may take an educated guess, I'm going to assume you can get us information we wouldn't ordinarily have access to. Am I right?"

"Bingo!" exclaimed Beryl, looking quite proudly at Ana.

"This will be quite helpful, Ana, and thank you for offering to assist us." Changing gears, Finch pompously proclaimed, "Now for the big announcement...I know what happened to Elizabeth's scarf!" He turned to look directly at Elizabeth as though he had just won the spelling bee. "I spoke with Officer Ruff this morning who told me Pastor White arrived late to the meeting and saw your scarf lying on the town hall floor. He picked it up, but when the brouhaha broke out with Ollie and Curtis, he forgot all about it and inadvertently put in his pocket and toted it back to the parsonage. He had planned to give it back to Elizabeth at the gala, but it went missing again before he had the chance to return it. The killer must have stolen it from Pastor White that night with the intent for his macabre dramatics. Thus, one mystery solved."

"You've got to be kidding. That doesn't even sound remotely plausible," said Elizabeth, shooting Finch a look that would have chilled an ice cube.

"That's because that's not true!" Ana said vehemently, as everyone turned toward her, stunned at her sudden outburst. "I saw exactly what happened, and it had nothing to do with Pastor White. The person who stole your scarf was..." Ana's voice dropped, terrified to continue.

Not a person stirred for fear of her fleeing.

"Ana, tell us what you know," Beryl gently urged, as she leaned over and patted Ana's arm.

"Go on, honey," Grace said, her voice calm and reassuring.

"I was sitting in the back of the hall when the argument between Mr. Williams and Mr. Hughes started. I could tell it was going to get super heated, and I got totally freaked out. So I slipped out of my seat and quietly made my way to the foyer to leave. That's when I noticed someone was digging through stuff around the coat rack. They were acting weird, you know, so I hid to see what they were up to. I could hear muffled noises like 'oohing' or something. When I took a chance and peeked around the corner, I saw them pull the scarf from the sleeve of

Mrs. Evans's red coat and stuff it in their pocket. They looked around like they were scared of getting caught red handed and made a mad dash out the door. I knew they had stolen that scarf, so I followed them to make sure it was who I thought it was."

"Well, who the devil was it?" asked Peg, impatient as always.

Ana gulped. "That new lady in town. The owner of the Holly Hill Inn."

"What? Virginia Pierce? I'm more confused than ever!" sputtered Elizabeth. "But what she said is true. I did run the scarf down the inside of my coat sleeve for safekeeping. A trick our mother taught us."

"This is certainly a twist I wasn't expecting," said Finch, ruminating. "If this is true..."

"It is true," said Ana emphatically and leaned forward, daring anyone to doubt her word.

"I believe you, Ana, and thank you for your courage. This was quite difficult for you, I'm sure, but I need to speak with Pastor White and get to the bottom of this. What would motivate a minister to lie about a theft? This is quite sobering," said Finch, sounding beleaguered.

"Yes, and you can bet I will speak to Virginia Pierce. No wonder she acted as if she saw a ghost when I tried to be friendly to her at the gala," Elizabeth inserted.

"I did see her chatting with the pastor that night, if that helps," inserted Peg. "There's something fishy going on with those two."

"The question is, did Virginia Pierce murder Wymark, or did someone else steal the scarf and then do the deed?" mused Beryl.

As soon as the conversational buzz dissipated, Finch, once again, took over to proceed. "Let's move on. Ana, can you do some snooping and find out what you can about Marshall Wymark?"

"Yes, Mr. Finch," Ana responded eagerly, delighted to be included so quickly.

"The man's certainly a mystery, and one we must solve because I think this is only a tiny piece to a much bigger puzzle. We may be in way over our heads," said Finch solemnly.

"My scarf is central to this puzzle, seeing as it was the murder weapon," reminded Elizabeth, to counter Finch's unwanted authority.

"Someone is going to have to confront Ollie, Curtis, and James about their altercation in the park," reminded Finch.

"I'll talk to James," said Grace. "He's always bothering me about selling my store, the piranha."

"I'll take Ollie," said Peg. "He's coming in tomorrow to pick up a book he ordered for the children's library. I sure hope he's not messed up in this."

"Good people do bad things," Finch responded. "Remember that. No one is as they seem."

"My, aren't we cynical!" smirked Elizabeth, facetiously. "Nothing like turning your friends into suspects."

"This *can't* be personal. We only go by the *facts*," said Finch decisively, reminding the group of the judge he once was.

"I want Virginia because this *is* personal for me," countered Elizabeth, "And I'll take Curtis too. Even if he thinks he's God's gift to all women. Pshaw."

"What are we going to do about telling Officer Ruff about our meddling?" asked Beryl.

"That will come in due time, ladies. Let's find out what we can first," responded Finch.

And with that, the small group made its way home with plenty to ponder.

7

The Interrogations

Early the next morning, Grace left her establishment to track down James Powell, the realtor. She was sure he would be in his office, no doubt scheming to take someone else's property at such a discount it was pure robbery. He lives in a palatial domicile very near Curtis Hughes. That part of town is referred to by most locals as the "swanky" section.

Grace was born and reared in North Falls, and as her mother, Seren Jones Morgan, liked to say, "We're as common as an old shoe." There were no airs in the Morgan clan. They were known for their honesty and integrity, and that meant the world to each of the sisters. As Seren would often say, "You're only as good as your word."

Well, thought Grace. Mr. Powell could take a lesson or two from my mother!

As she approached her destination, Grace couldn't help herself. She glanced toward the little village and marveled at the beauty of her birthplace. The town was pristine and decked out like a fairytale. The fresh snow glittered, resembling sugared glass, as it reflected the brilliant hues of holiday decorations like scattered rainbows dancing across the festive streets. Christmas would be upon them in no time, and she wanted to concentrate on the seasonal events she enjoyed. However, she and her fellow investigators had a murder, of all things, to solve. With that, she took a deep breath, opened the realtor's door, and entered.

"Oh, good morning! What can I do for you today?" asked Maggie Dolman, Powell's new receptionist. Maggie was a looker! She had long thick dark hair, rosy cheeks, plump lips, and dressed to kill. Grace thought she must be mysteriously related in some way to Elizabeth. Today she wore a pastel gray mohair sweater over a white boyfriend shirt, black pants and heels, matching pearl accessories, and dark rose lipstick. Maggie appeared to be friendly and likable, and for the life of her, Grace could not figure out why she worked for the property thief.

"Hello, dear. I don't believe I know you," said Grace, nonplussed. She thought she knew everyone in North Falls.

"Oh, hello. I'm Maggie. Mr. Powell's new secretary. Mrs. Therry retired."

"I was aware of that but didn't realize James had found a replacement. Well, it's nice to meet you, Maggie. I'm Grace Davis. By any chance is James in?" but before she took her next breath, James was at his door, practically begging her to come in.

"Right this way, Mrs. Davis. I hope you've changed your mind and are willing to sell Grace's Elegant Antiques and Furnishings. If so, this is my lucky day."

Grace didn't know whether to address his ridiculous question or offer him a hanky to wipe his drool. "No, I'm sorry, she's not for sale." Perhaps I should hand him a hanky. The little weasel looks as if he's about to cry, thought Grace. "This is about an entirely different topic."

"Oh, well, I must admit, I am most disappointed, but my offer is always on the table," he replied blithely.

A very small table, she thought.

James Powell was a tall, thin drink of water, always aspiring "to be someone." He married Blodwyn Powell, who came from an affluent family. Ole Blodwyn never let him forget where his bread and butter came from, and that was his motivation to prove his worth. He was losing his hair rather quickly, especially in the back where a shiny patch of skin seemed to grow wider each time Grace saw him. James had a long face, small teeth, and dark hair and eyes. His lips were thin and had a way of disappearing altogether when he smiled, as he was now. But that grin was about to vanish, as Grace proceeded with her assignment.

As was her way, Grace got right to the point as she took a seat and declined coffee. "I was wondering what you, Ollie Williams, and Curtis Hughes were arguing about in the park a few days ago? I understand it got quite heated."

Powell's face turned a brilliant shade of fuchsia as he sputtered, "What altercation?"

"Oh, you know, the altercation in the park, specifically in the children's play area. Someone saw the three of you about to go at each other's throats. What were you discussing that caused such an exchange, James?" Grace tried to hold his gaze, but he couldn't meet her eyes.

"I assure you, Mrs. Davis, I do not know what you're talking about. I did not meet Ollie or Curtis at any time. Your source must have me confused with someone else."

"Don't you drive a silver SUV with a magnetic Powell Realty placard on each door?" She waited patiently, like a cat ready to pounce. "Now, James, you and I both know that meeting took place, and you were there. Now, I want to know what the three of you were up to." One Mississippi, two Mississippi... "Did it, by any chance, have something to do with the new complex? Were you and Curtis trying to bully Ollie into taking your side?" Powell remained silent, as tiny beads of sweat broke out across his forehead. "You know I'll find out, so let's have it and stop wasting my time," demanded Grace in that demure way when she knows she has you.

"Mrs. Davis, once again, your source has got it wrong. That wasn't me," James replied a bit too panicky, which gave Grace the opportunity to swoop in for the kill.

"Not you, eh? My source has positively identified you, James, and Elizabeth Evans is never wrong," finished Grace smugly.

"Mrs. Evans?" he gulped.

"That's right, your former English teacher. Now, spill the beans."

And he did.

***

Across town, Finch was huffing and puffing up the freshly salted church steps in hopes of cornering Pastor White, who was not answering the parsonage door. In the early morning light, the church roof was dusted with pearls of newly fallen snow, as the sun beams caressed the glistening white. In the sacred silence, one could hear nearby cardinals singing their own versions of Christmas hymns.

Finch opened the wide wooden doors, each adorned with an elegant wreath of poinsettias, gold ornaments, and centered in the midst of it was the manager and the Christ child in fluorescent white. As he maneuvered himself through the foyer, he was overcome with the serene presence of something holy and quickly reminded himself of his mission. The entrance was decorated in sophisticated charm reminiscent of the sacred season. As he reverently entered the sanctuary, he was filled with a profound awe. Finch slowly took in the beauty that surrounded him and felt an old tug at his heart. It had been too long since he ventured into a place of such virtue. As he looked toward the altar, he saw Pastor White bowed in fervent prayer at the highly polished altar, totally oblivious to his presence.

"Excuse me, Pastor White. I'm so sorry to interrupt you while at prayer. May I have a word? It's quite important, concerning a certain *item*," said Finch ardently.

"Oh," stammered the minister as he clamored to his feet. "I didn't hear you enter. Let's go into my office where we can converse privately. Even these sacred pews have ears," he quietly whispered.

As they made their way to the side office, Pastor White looked as if he were headed to the gallows. He quickly closed the ornate door, offered Finch a comfortable seat, and asked if he would like a hot drink. After Finch declined, the steward of the North Falls Community Church began. "I'm sure you're here because of my story about Mrs. Evans's scarf."

"Right you are," answered the former judge with the stoicism of someone familiar with a confession.

"I really don't know how to proceed, so I'll just spit it out. I did not tell the truth."

And thus the confession began.

***

At the same time, not far away, Elizabeth entered the newly renovated Holly Hill Inn to receive her just dues. She stopped a pretty maid dressed in a uniform one would assume to see in a Victorian film. Her name tag read Macie, and she appeared in a hurry and quite flustered.

"Macie, could you please tell me where I can find Mrs. Pierce?"

"If it's important, she's through there," she said, nodding to a side office. "If not, you may want to come back later, when she's in a better mood," whispered the young maid.

"Oh, it's quite important. Thank you, young lady," answered Elizabeth, as she headed for the inn's office.

"It's your head," mumbled Macie as she turned and hurried away.

Elizabeth wanted to respond by saying, I may well have *her* head, but instead, knocked loudly on the door. The inn looked as grand as it did the night of the gala, but the ambience had changed. There was a distinct air of palpable tension.

"What?" came a gruff voice, filled with uppity intolerance.

Elizabeth opened the door and sashayed in, radiating confident authority.

"Good morning, Virginia," announced Elizabeth, smiling sweetly. "I hope you're having a grand day."

"Oh, Mrs. Evans. What a surprise." Virginia Pierce was clearly off her game and immediately came to her feet. The unexpected appearance of Elizabeth thoroughly unnerved her. "What can I do for you?"

"Let's just cut to the chase. You stole my scarf, and I want a reasonable explanation. I come from a long line of Welsh lineage, so the truth is very important to me." Wow, Elizabeth's voice ricocheted about the small office, and, to any bystander, it would be quite clear as to how she kept complete control of all those rowdy teenagers she previously taught. She was all business, and Virginia felt as if she were a sixteen-year-old about to be reprimanded.

"Oh, Mrs. Evans, I assure you it was quite by accident You see..."

"Let's start again, Mrs. Pierce, and this time *with the truth*. I have a very competent source who saw you take my scarf from the inside of my coat sleeve, looked about like the cat who just ate the canary, and fled town hall with my Christmas scarf stashed in your pocket. Now," said Elizabeth, counting on her fingers, "this is what I want to know. Why did you steal my scarf? How did it end up being a murder weapon, and why did Pastor White lie to protect you?" Elizabeth's voice rose slightly in exasperation. "...and who the heck is Marshall Wymark?"

Virginia Pierce sat down, hands trembling and tears welling, and slowly unraveled her story.

***

It was late morning when Elizabeth left the Holly Hill and headed to the bank to have her conversation with North Falls

Community Bank President Curtis Hughes. She was already pumping with excitement and in no mood for any more conniving denials. Elizabeth brazenly walked straight to the glassed-in office and, without knocking, caught Curtis totally by surprise. It's amazing what a senior citizen can get by with, thought Elizabeth. She intended to use every advantage to accomplish her mission.

Oh no, he thought, not Elizabeth Evans, but it was too late. She stood looking at him with such aplomb that he backed up and sat in his plush, and very expensive, chair, wishing he could slide under the desk and slither away. No such luck.

"Before you say anything," said Elizabeth, "I know about the argument in the park, so let's get right to it."

He hesitated, eyes darting away for a moment, before finally sinking back into his chair, defeated. Under Elizabeth's unwavering gaze, he had no choice but to submit to her scrutiny. The silence hung heavy between them, loaded with unspoken truths waiting to surface.

***

The tiny bell above the door of the old-fashioned bookshop gave warning to the intrusion of the expectant visitor who interrupted the stillness of the Bibliophile. Peg had been eagerly awaiting this liaison all afternoon, hoping to glean what she could from the imminent discussion with the elderly custodian, Ollie Williams.

"Greetings, Peg. I'm sorry I'm a little late, but I found a stray hound dog that was half starved to death. I just couldn't leave 'em until I filled his belly," confessed Ollie.

"Of course you did, Ollie. That's no surprise. How are you, my friend?"

"Fine as frog's hair, and you?"

"The same. Here's the book you ordered. I know the children will enjoy it. Come on back if you have time for a cup of tea, a fresh scone, and an old-fashioned chin wag," replied Peg. And off they went in search of two comfortable chairs and a much anticipated treat.

As they settled into the overstuffed chairs near the fireplace, comforted by towering shelves of books, Peg's voice dropped to a cautious whisper.

"Ollie, we need to discuss the squabble you had in the park. Elizabeth saw the whole thing," she said, gently broaching the sore subject.

A flicker of unease crossed Ollie's surprised face as he hesitated, scanning the quiet bookshop for any curious ears that might be tempted to eavesdrop. Panic clouded his tone.

"Oh dear," he said, taking a deep breath, eyes scanning the room again. His voice dropped to a low, urgent murmur. "When I met Curtis and James in the park, they offered me ten thousand dollars if I would vote for the expansion project."

Peg blinked, caught off guard. "Ollie, why? Why would they offer you that kind of money?"

He swallowed hard. "I can't reveal anything else about the project development. That's not up for discussion."

Abruptly, he rose from his chair, glancing at his watch. "It was a delight as always, Peg, but I'm afraid there's somewhere I must be."

From his sudden shift in demeanor, Peg had her suspicions that he was hiding something, because it still didn't explain the outburst Elizabeth witnessed at the park.

8

Another Reveal

J ust as the evening sun peeped beneath the wintry horizon, the novice detectives gathered at the Sugar Bowl. Beryl and Peg were busy serving the hungry investigators a hot, tasty supper prepared by Beryl and her staff. It was a much appreciated feast. Heaping plates of roast pork, dressing, mashed potatoes and gravy, creamed peas, and coleslaw were deftly placed in front of the hungry investigators. In the far corner, sat a medley of delectable desserts left over from the tiny restaurant's busy day. It did not take the small throng of ravenous chums long to devour the meal, as the hum of excitement pervaded throughout the homey dining area. As the chatter slowly dissipated, the anticipation of new information hung in the air, thick and heavy, waiting to be disclosed. Finch cleared his throat loudly,

"Ahem." The brusque sound broke the festive atmosphere, and the mundane chit-chat came to an abrupt end.

"Let's get started, shall we?" broached Finch, in his very judge-like voice.

Oh, thought Elizabeth, will he ever stop grandstanding?

"Who would like to go first?" Finch asked, looking expectedly at the sleuths.

"I'll go," said Grace. "I spoke with James Powell, as you all may remember. All I had to do was mention my source was Elizabeth, and he withered like the last flower of summer."

"Well, what did he say?" asked Peg.

"James said he and Curtis were trying to talk sense into Ollie who resisted with a vengeance. They tried to explain the perks the community would reap if the project goes though, but Ollie would hear none of it. It did get heated, and feeling the meeting was awash, they all left. He also denied knowing our murder victim. Oh, and he wanted to give Elizabeth his respectful regards."

"How honorable," Elizabeth responded a tad sarcastically. She much preferred Owen Rees to the sycophant, James Powell. "So, Grace, what was your assessment?"

"He's hiding something. I feel it in my bones. He told me just enough to verify Elizabeth's story, and that was it. Should I give him another visit?" She eagerly asked. "I don't mind. That was actually quite entertaining, watching him squirm."

"Let's wait to see how the other stories pan out. Next," said Finch.

"Well, I talked to Virginia Pierce and Curtis Hughes," replied Elizabeth.

"Let's stay on the same thread. First, what did you learn from Curtis?" questioned Finch.

"Interestingly enough, it was pretty much what Grace reported from her talk with James. I could tell right away he wasn't about to divulge a penny's worth of information he didn't have to. He emphatically denied knowing Wymark. But those questions? They threw him for a loop." Elizabeth paused, eyes narrowing.

"The liar," she muttered under her breath.

"Listen," she continued, "I know that man is somehow involved in this whole horrible nightmare, and I refuse to let him try to buffalo me with his innocent, cagy smile and perfect white teeth. He doesn't fool me for one minute. He will mess up, and when he does, I'll catch him like a fly on sticky tape! I hate it when men think they are so superior."

Grace looked at Finch and whispered loudly enough for all to hear, "She has a thing for men with perfect white teeth."

"Don't we all?" grinned Peg.

"You called him a liar, Elizabeth. Does that mean you think Hughes knows Wymark and is involved with his demise?" inquired Finch, as he leaned in toward Elizabeth as if she were the most interesting person in the room.

"Darn it, Finch. It's women's intuition! He may not be directly involved with Wymark, but he *is* connected in some way. I'm rarely wrong," intoned Elizabeth, as everyone shook their heads in agreement.

"She's right," spoke up Beryl, who had remained quiet for the duration of the meeting. "I am absolutely positive that Curtis is connected in this whole awful fiasco if Elizabeth says so."

"Ok, I'm not one to dispute a lady," began Finch.

"Humph!" interrupted Elizabeth.

"*but*," Finch continued, "we will have to prove it if we hope to solve this case successfully, and that is our goal. Isn't it?"

"Of course," said Grace, "but we've got a good starting point with the Morgan intuition."

"I agree with that," stated Beryl, quite businesslike.

"Now that we have established we are firm believers that Hughes and Powell are somehow involved, I would like to hear what Peg learned from her conversation with Ollie," directed Finch, staying focused and moving forward.

"Oh, he is such a dear, but he was surprised to learn that I knew about the quarrel in the park. I explained that Elizabeth was lurking nearby..."

"I wasn't *lurking*! I was sipping an herbal tea in the gazebo. *Lurking*!" scoffed Elizabeth, mildly offended at the use of Peg's choice of words.

"Sorry, *sipping* tea close by when she saw the whole thing," Peg said mockingly. Elizabeth was starting to worry Finch was rubbing off on her, too.

Peg then leaned in conspiratorially. "Get this...they offered him *ten thousand smackeroos* to vote for the project!"

"Ten thousand dollars! That development means that much to them that they'd bribe Santa? Preposterous!" gasped Beryl, her eyes wide with disbelief.

"Ten thousand dollars' worth of stench, you mean," Elizabeth mused, a frown creasing her brow. "Goodness, something must be pretty lucrative for those men to be willing to buy someone off with that kind of money. I wonder..."

"And that's not all," said Peg, eyes snapping. "He then abruptly left, letting me know the subject was off limits. I'm telling you, there's something he doesn't want anyone to know, and he's as scared as a deer in headlights."

"I knew it! As I stated before, there is something much bigger going on here than any of us realize," reminded Finch, as Elizabeth rolled her eyes theatrically.

"Now, Elizabeth," he said, his tone deliberate, "tell us what you ascertained when you spoke to Virginia Pierce this morning." His gaze remained fixed, fanatically focused on staying on topic, as the others were still reeling from hearing Ollie's revelation.

"She was easy and broke like a cheap China doll. I simply told her what we knew, and she didn't deny it. She did take the scarf and admitted that she is undergoing therapy because she is...Are you ready?" Elizabeth now paused for effect. "A bona fide kleptomaniac! Can't help herself. She sees something, she wants it, she takes it. Just think, if Ana hadn't actually seen her, she would never have been caught and who knows what else would have gone missing."

Just then Beryl noticed that Ana was not sitting at the table but was tucked away at the very back of the room, working diligently on her computer.

"Ana, are you all right, dear?" asked Beryl. There was no response.

Everyone began glancing around the room, looking for Ana, who sat hunched over her computer, eyes locked on the screen as her nimble fingers flew across the keyboard.

"Ana," Beryl repeated slightly louder, "are you all right?"

Suddenly aware that all eyes were on her, Ana looked up. "Oh, yes. Sorry. I'm in the zone. Be with you in a minute," she murmured.

"She must be onto something," said Finch. "Let's leave her to it."

Turning to face Elizabeth, Finch continued. "Interesting, Elizabeth. Anything else?"

"Yes, I questioned her as to how my scarf got tangled up as the murder weapon. She cried like a baby and assured me she had no idea. The plan was to have Pastor White return the scarf to me discreetly at the party, hoping I would be so happy to have it back that I wouldn't question the lame version they had cooked up and relayed to Officer Ruff. They had hidden it in her office drawer to keep it out of sight until the timing was right, but when Pastor White went to retrieve it, it had somehow vanished."

"Do you believe her?" Beryl asked intently, eagerly awaiting Elizabeth's valued opinion.

"Darn it, I do. It would be so convenient if we could clear this up so easily, but, yes, she was pretty convincing. I don't think she had anything to do with the murder," Elizabeth stated disappointedly but quickly added, "but keep your goods away from her! You've been forewarned."

"Did she know Wymark?" asked Grace.

"I didn't get the chance to ask her. She became so distraught for fear her husband would walk in, she begged me to leave. She gave a whole new meaning to the word histrionics. Don't worry. I'm not done with her yet." Elizabeth clicked her tongue and winked as she nodded her head.

"What's with her and the pastor, Finch?" asked Peg, hoping he was going to give them a racy little tidbit.

"Yes, well, ahem, this was a most interesting conversation. He admitted on the spot that he did, in fact, lie."

Everyone gasped, as Peg said, "I knew it! There was something off about them at the gala. It was as if they were two scared rabbits in MacGregor's garden, afraid of getting caught with a carrot. I'm telling you, there is a lot more going on with those two than meets the eye."

"I agree with you both," said Finch. "There is something else going on with those two. I don't have the intuition all of you have, but my gut tells me the same thing. Ana, can I have your attention for a moment?"

"Yes," she called across the room. "What is it, Mr. Finch?"

"I want to give you another task, if I may. Research Ed and Virginia Pierce and our illustrious new pastor, John E. White. *E* for Ellsworth. His last parish was somewhere in Illinois."

I'll get right to it as soon as I finish this. Don't fret, I'll find them."

"So, Finch, did you discover anything else about Pastor White, or is that it?" asked Elizabeth, smugly.

"John White said he was acquainted with Virginia and Ed before any of them moved here, but refused to say more. He said he was sorry for the untruth, but he was trying to save Virginia from undue humiliation. Although he said that is not a feasible excuse, he is ashamed of his behavior and promised to be more forthcoming in the future if anything like this happens again."

"Did you believe him?" asked Elizabeth.

"The jury's still out. No pun intended," smiled the former judge.

At last, Ana joined them, and her demeanor caused them all to pause.

"She's definitely found something," whispered Grace. "She's as animated as Jack when he found the giant's goose that laid the golden egg."

"What's with you guys and the kiddy stories?" Elizabeth asked, amused at their literary examples.

"So, Ana, do you have something to report about Marshall Wymark?" Finch asked, ever keeping the meeting on track and keen to know what information she may have uncovered.

"Yes," stated Ana confidently, pausing as if waiting for her drumroll. Dear me, thought Elizabeth, we are all turning into miniature Finches.

"The individual called Marshall Wymark...does *not* exist."

"What?" gasped Peg, hardly believing what she was hearing.

"What in the world does that mean?" Elizabeth responded sharply. She was tired from being so wired up all day with the interviews, and now that her stomach was full, and her information divulged, topped off with the toasty feel of the room, all she wanted was to go home and cuddle with her little hound.

"As I've told you, I am very good at finding people or anything for that matter." Ana began enunciating each word clearly and slowly for the shock to set in, as she knew it would. "Marshall Wymark does *not* exist."

"What exactly do you mean 'he doesn't exist'?" Finch prodded, as his words cut through the tension. His excitement was palpable. His eyebrows were twitching like two rabid caterpillars.

"Marshall Wymark is *not* who he said he was," Ana said, her voice sharp. "There's literally nothing about this guy anywhere, and trust me, I searched everywhere. My guess? Either he's a genius at totally wiping his identity off the internet, or someone else is doing it for him. That guy was out there pretending to be some big-shot author with this amazing literary background, but he hasn't even *published* a single book. Whoever made up this whole story is seriously good at it, and I kind of want to know who they are. But...I'm *not* gonna let them pull one over on me. I'll figure out who this guy really was," Ana proclaimed, as her eyes narrowed. The game was on! Her determination to uncover Wymark's identity and her competitive hunger to win were written all over her face.

"But he said he was an author of horror fiction. I distinctly remember his saying that at the gala," contemplated Grace, as she sat back and crossed her arms.

"Yes, you're right," declared Peg. "I remember his saying that, too. I even looked him up on Facebook."

"All his social media platforms are fakes and professionally done," Ana responded with unwavering conviction.

"So why is there nothing on him? Finch, any ideas?" asked Elizabeth.

Finch was so surprised that Elizabeth had actually asked him a legitimate question, he literally looked as if he would fall off his seat. Quickly recovering, he answered, "Yes, I think I do, but I want to converse with Ana before I say anything more. Let's retire for the night and reconvene tomorrow at six at Grace's."

"Well, I won't have anything as elaborate as Beryl or Peg, but I'll have some refreshments, just don't expect much," answered Grace truthfully.

"No, it's fine. We'll meet back here tomorrow. It will be easier for me anyway." Ah, yes, Beryl who always tries to help out and smooth over. And with that, the weary private eyes once again headed for home.

When Grace split off from the others to return to her home, Finch and Elizabeth were left walking alone. Suddenly Elizabeth stopped and turned to face the illustrious judge. "Finch, I've been thinking. Curtis's jewelry theft... something's off. A murder *and* a jewelry theft all at once in a tiny village? It just doesn't sit right."

"Well, to be honest, I've been so immersed in organizing this whole investigation, I must have let my mind slip on a few oddities, but I do agree. Something doesn't smell right. Let me walk you home."

"No, that's not necessary. I wouldn't want someone who is so forgetful to walk me home, and then forget where he is. It must be your age," grinned Elizabeth. It was a playful jab, and they both realized the game for what it was, and yet the underlying message was clear. Elizabeth was setting her boundaries. She did not want him walking her home or getting any ideas. She was not interested in a relationship, and if that were where he was headed, she intended to head him off at the pass. "Good night, Finch."

As Elizabeth began to turn onto her street, Finch couldn't let her have the last word. "I may be getting older, but I bet I'm not as old as you, pretty lady," and with a sultry wink and a smile, he was gone.

"Pretty lady, indeed," she scoffed, but she couldn't help noticing how good looking he was under the Victorian lamplight on a snowy evening in the most perfect village in the world.

9

Trouble

I t was decided the night before that Finch was the best person to skillfully fill in Officer Ruff on what they knew, making it sound as though it wasn't meddling, just concerned citizens passing on what they deemed helpful information. As Finch left the police station, he headed for his day job at the Welsh Cupboard. Ah, he felt lucky to have found this little community. It seemed the ugliness of the world had not yet penetrated the village, that is until the dastardly deeds of recent. His thoughts then turned to Elizabeth. What was so intriguing about her? She could be so dang annoying with her self-assured opinions and overly confident demeanor, but she was such a striking woman. Downright beautiful, he thought. He so wanted to ask one of the Morgan sisters about the mystery of Elizabeth's ex-husband to ascertain if he were the cause of her vehement disdain against his gender, but it seemed a topic no one dared speak of. After getting to know the Welsh women, he deemed airing one's uncomfortable past was definitely crossing a private family boundary. Well, he would just have to do some snooping on his own. Ana was proving herself to be quite an asset. He had given her some very classified directions in which to pursue the enigmatic Wymark. He knew, if his assumption were correct, she would find the elusive information. She promised not to reveal anything she discovered with the others until she spoke with him first. He believed he could trust this girl. She wanted so very badly to please. Perhaps he could ask her to dig up some information on the infamous Mr. Samuel Evans but decided not to push his luck, at least not yet. One of his fellow sleuths could also ask Ana for a favor, probably Elizabeth, and he certainly didn't want anyone digging into his past for fear of discovering his own dark secret.

***

It was a brilliant day. The clouds were dancing in the sky, and the temperature was tolerable, as long as one wore the proper attire. Wonderful aromas permeated the streets as bakers and candymakers cast off their colorful creations in tantalizing window displays to lure tourists and locals alike into their establishments. Honestly, who could resist? The forecast predicted dropping temperatures and more snow as the evening approached, but for now, it was a perfect day to do a bit of sleuthing and make it back to the warm comfort of one's home before the snow made another appearance.

Grace left her shop to venture out in the hope of catching James Powell in his office. She wanted to question him about his purposeful omission of the wad of cash he promised if Ollie were to switch sides in favor of the abominable shopping center and all it promised in the way of "community advancement."

Grace opened the door so boldly, Maggie Dolman jumped, as cold air pushed its way into the small foyer. She looked stunning today in a raspberry Angora sweater, matching shoes, gray slacks, and bold gold jewelry. Her long hair was worn in a trendy ponytail that accentuated her subtle makeup and magenta lips. "Oh, Mrs. Davis, you nearly scared me to death. Two visits in two days. How lovely," she smiled. "Mr. Powell's in if you need to talk with him again. I'll just buzz him to let him know you're back."

"Don't bother, dear. I'll just be a moment," as Grace very deliberately made her way to the office door, opened it with the same boldness, and entered to find James in deep conversation with, none other than, Mayor Beeman. "Oh dear, I hope I'm not interrupting anything, but, James dear, I need to speak to you about an urgent matter." She was not about to wait in the adjoining room to give them time to concoct a convenient story. Something was up, she was sure of it.

The politician looked like a man who had just been caught with his hand in the cookie jar. "Oh, oh, Mrs. Davis. I was just finishing up," a frazzled Mayor Beeman said, trying to compose himself. "I may be looking for a new house and just stopped in to see if there were any new listings. You don't know of any, do you?"

"Gracious no, Mayor. Mr. Powell is the one who knows a great deal of what goes on in this little town. He'd be the one to ask. Isn't that right, James?" Grace purred.

Before James could answer, Mayor Beeman grabbed his coat and hat and made to skedaddle before Grace could inquire anything more about his conference with James. "I'll leave you to it then. And, James, you hear of anything, let me know. Nice seeing you, Mrs. Davis."

But Grace sensed the "let me know" was nothing concerning new houses on the market.

The office door clicked with an urgency as Beeman made a hasty retreat out the private back entrance, and James looked none too pleased to see Grace invading his premises, yet again. "What brings you back?" asked James. Gone was the timidity and intimidation from yesterday. His tone alluded to something altogether different today. Perhaps fear?

"Well, let's get right to it then," said Grace and took a seat that was not offered, much to James's discontent.

"I really don't have much time, Mrs. Davis," James answered, just a tad curtly to show his displeasure, yet keeping his tone civil and respectful.

"Absolutely. Why didn't you tell me yesterday that you and Curtis offered Ollie a whopping ten thousand dollars for him to come over to your side? I don't want to sound presumptuous, James, but it seems to me you omitted that little tidbit deliberately."

"Who told you that? That's pure fiction," stammered James, melting rapidly under Grace's penetrating gaze.

"Poppycock, James. Are you expecting me to believe that good ole Ollie would lie? For if you are, stop it right now. What's going on, and don't leave anything out this time."

But James had nothing more to add, as his hands began to tremble, betraying his bravado, saying nothing of his dancing feet.

Well, Grace thought as she exited the building, he had his chance. It's time for plan B, and off she went to the "swanky" part of town.

***

Sycamore Circle is a posh neighborhood in North Falls that showcases neatly manicured lawns and pristine homes adorned with the latest holiday décor, transforming the tranquil street into a magical winter wonderland. One neighborhood couple even broadcasts their own AM radio station, filling the air with classic Christmas tunes so visitors can soak in the holiday cheer as they gawk at the opulent and lavish displays. Each house seems to outdo the next, decked out in a spectacular show of twinkling lights, glowing reindeer, and towering Yuletide characters. Families from all over the county make the trek to bask in the Christmas magic, where neighbors joyfully compete to create the most dazzling outdoor holiday spectacle.

Grace, wrapped in a thick winter coat, gently knocked on the door, smiling as she took in the festive Christmas display that framed James and Blodwyn Powell's front porch. The door opened to reveal Blodwyn, a plain, simply dressed woman with curly brown hair, a double chin, and a friendly demeanor. Because of her frumpy appearance, no one would ever guess she came from such an affluent background.

"Grace! It's so nice to see you. Come on in!" Blodwyn said, greeting her unexpected visitor.

"I'll only stay a few minutes," responded Grace in a courteous tone, for the news she was about to drop may cut her visit short.

Grace stepped into the warmly lit foyer, greeted by lush pine garlands woven with white lights and trimmed with red and gold bulbs, cascading elegantly over the banister and doorframe in a radiant holiday exhibition.

Blodwyn immediately offered refreshments, but Grace was on a mission and this was no time to dally. They both took a seat on a lemon-hued sofa covered in soft buttery accent pillows. As the two women made themselves comfortable, Grace braced herself for a possible confrontation, unsure how Blodwyn would react to the disconcerting news.

"I don't know quite how to say this, but are you aware that James and Curtis Hughes met Ollie Williams in the park and offered him ten thousand dollars if he would vote for the expansion project?"

The warm smile vanished from Blodwyn's face, replaced by a look of dismay. "No, I had no idea..." she whispered, her voice trembling slightly.

Grace took a deep breath, steadying herself. "I thought you should know. If that expansion project passes, it could change the dynamics of the whole town."

Blodwyn's eyes narrowed, a flicker of anger mixed with disbelief. "Why would they do such a thing? It's...it's a betrayal. James knows I am adamantly against the mall. I can't believed he went behind my back."

Grace nodded solemnly.

"It will be a disaster if that thing passes. That's what it'll be!" barked Blodwyn.

"So you don't have any idea where the money came from?" Grace asked, her tone curious, but cautious.

"Absolutely not, and it better not have been from James!" Blodwyn snapped, clearly irritated with her husband.

"I'm sorry to have been the bearer of bad news," Grace said, the weight of the conversation heavy on her tongue. It pained her to discuss such a touchy issue. She carefully told Blodwyn the story beginning with Elizabeth's scarf and concluding with James's elusive comments.

"Don't you worry, Grace. I'll get to the root of it. You can bet your bottom dollar on that," Blodwyn said, her chin set in determination.

After polite goodbyes, Grace departed from the swanky part of town with a smirk upon her face. Take that, James Powell. I'm afraid you're in for a rough night tonight!

***

Elizabeth was retracing her steps from yesterday as well. She entered through the heavy metal-and-glass doors into a spacious room with soaring ceilings and ornate architectural details. The bank exuded an air of old-world finance. Marble cashier counters gleamed beneath bronzed-antique light fixtures, and stern portraits of former North Falls' former magnates lined the walls near Hughes's office. Curtis was nowhere to be seen, probably "out" due to an important appointment, a phone call from James, no doubt. Elizabeth marched herself over to Judith, one of the many bank tellers and one she had taught years ago. Judith Frazier was a plump woman in her early forties with frizzy blond hair pulled away from a kind face with a silver barrette and wearing a subdued lavender sweater set adorned with tiny pearls that had seen its better days.

"Good morning, Judith," she said pleasantly. "How are the boys, Tommy and Timmy."

"They're growing like weeds. Tommy's in fifth grade now, and Timmy's in third. I can't keep them in shoes," laughed Judith, clearly pleased Mrs. Evans remembered her sons' names. "What can I do for you today?"

"I wanted to talk with Curtis. Do you know when he's expected back?"

"He should be in his office. I just saw him," said Judith, as she craned her neck, surprised to find he was no longer there. "That's funny. Maybe he just stepped out."

"Judith, it's really important I speak with him. How about you call me when he comes back," winked Elizabeth.

"Our secret?" Judith winked back conspiratorially.

"Just like in a James Bond movie."

"How exciting!" exclaimed Judith, playing along.

"Here's my cell number. Thank you, Judith, and get those boys some new shoes," smiled Elizabeth, and off she went to revisit Virginia Pierce.

Not five minutes later, her phone began to hum "Have Yourself a Merry Little Christmas" as an unfamiliar phone number appeared on the screen.

"Hello?"

"Mrs.Evans?" responded a voice in a shaky whisper.

"Who is this, please?"

"Oh, I'm sorry. It's Judith, from the bank."

"Why do you sound so nervous, Judith?"

"Oh, do I? It's just that Mr. Hughes saw us talking and wasn't at all happy. He made it abundantly clear that I was to tell you that the next time you stopped by, he would be 'too busy' to see you."

"But I thought he was out. He's returned, then?" probed Elizabeth.

"I think he was hiding from you. But I did learn he's meeting a client for a luncheon at the Holly Hill in a little while. Maybe you could *accidentally* run into him there? I mean that's a pretty popular lunch spot, isn't it?" replied Judith coyly. "Just keep it under your hat, Mrs. Evans."

"Don't you worry about that, dear. It will be our little secret. Have a good day, and, Judith, thank you so much."

"Mrs. Evans, you were the best teacher I ever had. You be careful. Mr. Hughes is not in a good mood," warned Judith.

"You're a doll," said Elizabeth, and ended the call. He's hiding from me. I must have hit a nerve! thought Elizabeth excitedly. Now we're getting somewhere, and off she went to have a heart-to-heart with the community klepto.

***

Macie, the young maid who had warned Elizabeth on her last visit about Virginia's dark mood, was nowhere to be seen today, as Elizabeth made her way to the Holly Hill Inn's office. As she opened the door, there was Virginia seated at her desk, looking quite distraught, and standing next to her, with his hand on her shoulder, was Pastor White. "Oh, I guess I should have knocked. What's going on?" asked Elizabeth, as she frowned at the awkward scene.

"It's not what you think," stammered the good minister and dropped his hand as if he had been scalded.

"Of course not," Elizabeth said, solicitously.

Virginia was quick to react. "I was so upset after our discussion yesterday that I got all worked up in a panic. I mean, what if the killer is after me next because I took that darn scarf? I called Pastor White, and he came over to try to calm me down." Virginia was so overwrought and hiccuping to beat the band that it was difficult to understand her.

"That's right. She's in a terrible state. I'm sure Mr. Finch told you everything. I apologized for what I did. I'm sorry about all of it, but then, a murder on top of it! It's pushed Virginia over the edge, I'm afraid," the reverend spoke dolefully, looking down at Virginia, who was still hiccuping heavily. "In fact, it's my fault entirely. I should have advised Virginia to come straight to you with the scarf and confess. You seem to be a trustworthy person and are much valued in the community. We both made mistakes, but Virginia had nothing to do with the murder, nor did I."

"Why didn't you, Pastor?" asked Elizabeth.

"Why didn't I what?"

"Why didn't you advise Mrs. Pierce to simply return my scarf? I'm a forgiving woman, Reverend, and then my scarf would not have been used to take Mr. Wymark's life."

"I can't really answer that," the minister said.

"Who invited Mr. Wymark to the gala?" Elizabeth asked, abruptly changing the subject. Her brusque manner sometimes made Elizabeth seem a bit harsh or aloof, but she was the sort to get to the root of a problem, solve it, and move on.

"I have no idea. I'd never seen him before in my life. He said he was a famous author. I was busy making sure everything went smoothly. I was nervous since it was our introduction into the community, and I wanted everything to be perfect. I honestly didn't think any more about him," Virginia whined, looking quite miserable.

"I've never met him before either. I'm new to the area, as you know, and have yet to meet everyone," joined in the pastor.

"Who was the poor man, Mrs. Evans?" asked Virginia between sniffles.

"I have no idea, but you can bet on one thing. I'm going to find out. No one is going to plant my scarf at a murder scene, point the blame in my direction, and get away with it." And out the door she flew when Curtis Hughes literally ran smack dab into her. The look on his face said it all. "Oh, Curtis, I'm so glad...we bumped into each other," laughed Elizabeth, who politely took him by the arm and guided him back to the office she had just vacated.

There stood Virginia and the minister, engaged in their own private conversation, both turning to stare at the intruders with genuine looks of surprise on their faces. As Pastor White made his excuse to leave, Virginia sank back heavily into her chair.

"Virginia, you don't mind us using your office for a bit, do you? We'll just be a minute. Thank you, dear," Elizabeth said with her usual unshakable poise.

It's amazing how people just do whatever Elizabeth tells them. Without a word, Virginia automatically rose from her seat and exited without a word. Elizabeth closed the door, then turned toward Curtis, "Have a seat. This won't take long."

"What do you want, Mrs. Evans? I am..."

"a very busy man. Yes, I know," replied Elizabeth, cutting him off. "Why did you and James Powell offer Ollie Williams ten thousand dollars to back the shopping mall complex? And why didn't you mention that before?"

"I..." began Curtis.

"don't know what I'm talking about," finished Elizabeth. "We both know you're very aware of the fact that I know about the proposition. I need answers now, Curtis. Murder is a serious issue," concluded Elizabeth.

"Murder? What in blue blazes are you talking about, Mrs. Evans? Have you not been feeling well, or perhaps you're lonely and need a purpose after retiring from all those belligerent high school kids?" Curtis Hughes did not attend North Falls High School. He attended a private school on the East coast and only returned to North Falls years later to fill his retired father's vacancy as the head honcho at the bank. Otherwise, he would have known that it is not wise to speak to Elizabeth Evans so discourteously.

Elizabeth was rankled by his unkind remarks. "Don't get smart with me, Curtis, or I'll have a little talk with Officer Ruff, and we'll see what he thinks about the situation."

Hughes looked shell-shocked but recovered nicely. "You talk to whomever you want, Mrs. Evans. But Ruff will most likely come to the same conclusion as I have. Now I must be going," and got up as if to leave.

"How is your jewelry theft coming along?" asked Elizabeth.

That stopped the insufferable banker in his tracks. "What do my missing jewels have anything to do with this?"

"Don't you think it's a bit uncanny that a jewelry theft *and* a murder were committed in this itty-bitty little town?"

"I told you I do not know this Wymark character, and any conversations I have with Mr. Williams are strictly confidential, but here it is," he replied exasperated. "This project can change this community and provide employment to keep North Falls on the map. That's all I care about, preserving this little village so our grandkids and their grandkids can enjoy it as well. If you can't see it, perhaps you need to speak to our young folks as I have. No jobs, no chance of advancement, no North Falls. And once again, my jewels have nothing to do with Mr. Wymark and his murder or the project. Satisfied?"

He looked at Elizabeth pointedly. "And don't make any more surprise visits to my office. Do you understand?" Hughes spouted quite emphatically.

"Am I satisfied with your lecture, Curtis? No. You aren't civic-minded enough to care about the future of this village. I've known about your greedy appetite, as well as everyone else who has ever lived in North Falls. Go ahead and spew all this ridiculous trash and see what sticks to the wall. But something is amiss, and we both know it. Furthermore, I will find out what's going on. Do you understand?"

"Mrs. Evans, did Ollie say whether or not he accepted the ten thousand dollars?"

"Oh, come on, Curtis. He didn't need to. Ollie is a man of integrity. He would never accept a bribe from you or anyone else," letting her tone and cadence carry the message that Hughes was not, in her opinion, a man of integrity.

And with that, the president of the North Falls Community Bank slammed the door and exited the inn, leaving Elizabeth Evans whopping mad.

***

After a long and busy day at Grace's Antiques & Furnishings, Grace's shoulders slumped with exhaustion as she sat on a padded stool, tallying the day's receipts while Ivy Campbell, her assistant, rang up the last customer. Ivy was a retired third-grade teacher who had recently lost her beloved husband Finn and desperately needed something to keep her mind occupied. Grace's former employee, Joyce Collins, had retired and moved to Clearwater, so she approached Ivy with the job offer, and she happily accepted. The arrangement worked out well for both of them. Ivy is as honest as the day is long, and Grace loves their afternoon tea breaks and chats at the end of the day.

"Another lucrative day," said Ivy, "and I'm bushed. I'm going to check the new inventory in the back, dust a bit, and head out."

"You can do that in the morning. I'm wiped out too," replied Grace. "Ivy, before you go, how well do you know Blodwyn Powell?"

"The realtor's wife? She's in my book club and a real corker. She keeps James in line, let me tell you. She definitely wears the pants in that family."

"That's exactly the impression I got," said Grace, recalling her conversation with Blodwyn earlier that afternoon. Blodwyn got so worked up at one point, Grace was ready to call 911 while mentally reviewing CPR steps. Thank goodness she didn't have a stroke.

"I'm going to grab my coat and head out then," replied Ivy. As she made her way to the storage room, she saw something that took her breath.

"Grace, can you come here?"

As Grace appeared, she immediately saw what had astounded Ivy. Someone had been in the backroom and left a nasty calling card. On her newly acquired Chippendale desk was a message scrawled in red paint across its immaculate surface. Grace was more devastated to see such a magnificent piece of art so purposely ravaged, as she was the admonition of the message. "Call Officer Ruff, Ivy, and report the break-in and vandalism. Ask him to come over, and then you can go on home."

"I'm not leaving you alone," Ivy said as she hurried to make the call.

Forty minutes later, Officer Ruff had taken statements from Ivy and Grace, checked the shop and the outside area, and promised to send a patrol car around periodically to ensure the property remained free of any more damaging tactics. He surmised that someone had entered undetected through the delivery door and left an emphatic declaration. Ivy left once the sisters arrived.

"What low life would do something as evil as this?" complained Peg.

"It has to have something to do with this murder mess," bemoaned Beryl. "Perhaps we need to back off and let the police handle it from here on out."

"Absolutely not!" Elizabeth emphatically stated. "We're making someone very nervous, which means we're on the right track. We can't stop probing now. Onward!"

"Onward!" they all shouted as the message, OLD BONES SNAP EASY, loomed before them.

***

It was late evening when Elizabeth finally walked Grace home and got her settled. Grace was indeed a tough old bird, but Elizabeth could tell the whole ordeal had her rattled. She thought about calling Finch to fill him in on the incident but then thought better of it. She also considered asking if he would check to make sure her house was untouched by vile hands but decided that was a can of worms she was not yet ready to open, if ever.

As Elizabeth neared her home, she noticed that not only was her front door damaged, but it was standing wide open! What in the world? And then it hit her, the fear, that horrible paralyzing fear that gripped the most fragile part of her heart. Abner! Would someone stoop so low as to harm her dog? If someone would threaten Grace with such destruction, then yes, Abner would be a trivial loss for the vermin who threatened Grace and despoiled her exquisite inventory. Elizabeth ran breathlessly from room to room, becoming lightheaded. She raced upstairs flinging doors open, peering under beds, searching closets, frantically looking everywhere and calling out to her beloved companion. Her heart was beating so violently she thought she would pass out. Elizabeth's palms became sweaty, and her forehead prickled with the inkling of an oncoming anxiety attack. The stark realization sank in. Abner was *not* in the house. She knew it, *felt* it, even before she entered her residence. No sweet welcome, no precious tail wagging. They've taken my dog, she thought, and with that single, shattering truth, the tough-as-nails exterior crumbled at last.

Without thinking twice, she grabbed her cell, hit speed dial, and briefly waited for her friend to pick up. It had taken but two shakes of a lamb's tail for him to appear, as she hastily retold the scary events of the evening. As Finch listened intently, there was a light knock at the door.

"Elizabeth?" came a kindly voice from the porch. There in the downy glow from the lampposts, stood the sweetest little creature imaginable. She was dressed in a heavy dark green jacket revealing a striped pink and white winter nightgown under- neath as though she had dressed quickly. Her legs were shielded from the cold in long woolly socks tucked inside dark Welling- ton boots as though she were ready to go duck hunting. Her benign face radiated a life well lived and was as wizened as an old tree trunk. Her brown eyes snapped at the peril she witnessed earlier.

"Mrs. Edwards? What on earth are you doing out there?" asked Elizabeth. The snow was starting to fall as promised, and the temperature had already dropped below freezing.

"Your dog was makin' the awfullest racket ever was and run- ning up and down the street. I thought for sure he was goin' git hit," she said.

"Where is he? Is he all right?" Elizabeth asked breathlessly.

"I called for him twice, and the little thing came hightailing it in as fast as his little feet would go. He was acting all high and mighty like he was the neighborhood watchdog. Hee hee. I took him in my house so he wouldn't get into any more trouble," Mrs. Maude Edwards touted proudly, as if she had saved the day, and, in fact, she had. "It was a man," she whispered darkly.

"What?"

"It was a man in a long black coat and a funny-looking hat that broke into your house. Sort of looked like that new preacher over at Community. He ran like a scalded dog when I yelled at him. I guess anyone who would break in on a single woman is the devil. You all right now? I bet that scared the bejesus out of you," the affable neighbor said. "I'll go get Abner and bring you some blackberry wine to settle you down. I make it myself. I have a little swig every night," she snickered. "You look like you could use it."

"I just need my dog, Mrs. Edwards. I promise we'll have a nightcap another evening, if that's alright?" Elizabeth could have fallen to her knees with relief, but she held herself steady so as not to give away an inkling of weakness to Finch.

Mrs. Edwards returned quickly as she rounded the porch with Abner leading the way, as if he were the only one who knew the way home. Elizabeth scooped her little hound into her arms. She was covered in canine kisses and thanked her neighbor profusely.

"Oh, I almost forgot to give you this." Mrs. Edwards pulled a crumpled paper from her jacket pocket. "Your intruder must have dropped this on your porch step when I caught him up to no good. If I'd been younger, I could have caught him myself. I always won the 100-meter dash," she chuckled. "Coward!" Mrs. Edwards muttered under her breath as she made her way back to the warm safety of her home.

Again, Officer Ruff made his way to the second strange incident that evening in the sleepy little village. After Elizabeth explained what had happened, she handed over the tattered message found on her doorstep. OLD BONES SNAP EASY, the exact words scribbled in red across the intricate desk Grace had been so proud to acquire. Officer Ruff insisted on taking fingerprints. Fingerprints in North Falls? Elizabeth was astounded at the village police's current technology.

"Mrs. Evans," began Officer Ruff. "Why do you think someone would vandalize Mrs. Davis's store and then target you all on the same night?"

"How about Mrs. Evans and Mrs. Davis join you tomorrow morning at the police station, say, 9 o'clock? They can answer all your questions then. It seems the ladies have had quite the evening. Don't you agree?" persuaded the former judge.

Finch to the rescue!

"If that's all right with you, Mrs. Evans?" Officer Ruff asked gently.

"Yes, I am quite exhausted," replied Elizabeth.

"I'm going to take another look around your premises before I go and then see you in the morning. If you hear or see anything out of kilter, you call me immediately. Night, folks." Officer Ruff, careful not to let his anxiety show for fear of upsetting

Elizabeth even more, was in a tizzy. His brain was working furiously, and he knew that there was much not being said. No bother. He would interrogate the sisters and others who may possibly be involved soon enough, knowing he would get to the bottom of it. That was why he was so good at his job. But what really niggled at him was the strange series of crimes, and why Elizabeth Evans always seemed to be at the center of it. As the policeman circled the premises, a chilling question nagged at him. What had two senior citizens done to earn such menacing warnings that promised unforeseen danger?

After Finch thoroughly checked the house once again, upstairs and down, Elizabeth rejected his suggestion that she spend the night at Beryl's, and he left, promising to call her bright and early in the morning. Elizabeth, Grace, and Finch would have an in-depth discussion to go over details before their trek to the station. Finch wanted them to be prudent about what to reveal and what not to expose until their investigation was back on track. Once Finch did his deed to ensure that Elizabeth was safe, he cast off into the night, promising to call Grace and fill her in. At last, Elizabeth crawled into bed, and for the first time, she lifted her little beagle onto the big four-poster cherry bed and tucked him under the comforter next to her. They slept like stones.

10

The Plot Thickens

The meeting at the police station wasn't quite as gnarly as the Morgan sisters had anticipated. They decided the best avenue was the honest one, so they answered the officer's questions truthfully. That wasn't to say they divulged any extra information, but each felt she had done her civic duty. After receiving an emphatic admonishment from Ruff about their safety, they were off to regroup after breakfast. Neither sister was looking forward to that. Once Beryl and Peg heard the latest frightening developments, they knew they were in for it.

***

Finch had wanted to march over to Powell's and Hughes's offices and have it out but acquiesced to the group's more sensible suggestions.

"I don't think they did it," stated Beryl confidently.

"What?" came a chorus of nonbelievers.

"You can't be serious," railed Elizabeth. "Who else would have motivation?"

"First of all, I think we all need to take a deep breath and start scrutinizing the information we have available, and then plan our next step. A chat with Ollie is foremost to see if he confirms or denies accepting the bribe, even though we all agree he would never do such a thing. Next, we need to ask Pastor White if he did, in fact, visit Elizabeth's last night and to what purpose. Then,"continued Beryl, "we meet back here at closing and see where we are."

"Why do you think that cad Hughes and the rat Powell are innocent?" asked Peg.

"It doesn't sit right. It's as if someone is deliberately trying to make it look as if Curtis and James are the culprits setting Elizabeth up and then terrorizing her and Grace, which is mighty cruel, I might add." Beryl took another deep breath and continued, nervously picking a stray thread on her spotless apron.

"They aren't the only ones who have a vested interest in this dang development, so I suggest we cast our net further out to sea. Understand, I'm not letting them off the hook, but so far, they are only guilty of pushing the dreaded community project. Curtis's mother's missing jewels are a whole other scenario. Let's hold it there until we meet later." Her calm demeanor couldn't hide the rising storm behind her eyes.

"Agreed. Where's Ana?" asked Finch, looking around. "I've got a question for her."

"Oh, I forgot. She wants you to meet her at the library media room. She has it reserved," replied Beryl.

"I don't think it's a good idea for any of you girls to approach either of our suspects. It's too risky," contemplated Finch. "Let me speak with Ana. Peg, you round up Ollie and invite him to our meeting this evening so we can all talk to him here. After I see Ana, I'll run over to the parsonage to have another word with John."

"So what are we supposed to do? Sit here and twiddle our thumbs? I want some answers too, and I'm not afraid to get my hands dirty," spouted Elizabeth, who was still fuming over the terror she experienced last night.

"Elizabeth, I'm upset too, but we were both overly aggressive with our assignments. Let's just step back and regroup later, as Beryl suggested. She is a Pisces," reminded Grace.

"Class dismissed," said Peg, bringing the meeting to a close, but Elizabeth was having none of it. She was going to confront Curtis if it were the last thing she did.

***

Later that day, Elizabeth parked her car across the street from the North Falls Community Bank, waiting to confront her nemesis, Curtis Hughes, as he left for the day. If he wouldn't see her during working hours, well, there was more than one way to skin a cat. Suddenly, the back door opened and out poured the bank employees, led by none other than her partner-in-crime, Judith. Once the gaggle of employees had departed, it was another forty-five minutes until the door finally opened once again as...Mayor Beeman emerged! Following right on his tail was Curtis, who quickly locked and checked the heavy door. He and the aging politician walked slowly to the employees' parking lot, pausing by Hughes's Mercedes, as it gleamed like burnished glass in the frosty light. What in the world would the mayor and Curtis have to discuss? Maybe a community expansion project? How infuriating! Beeman is supposed to be on the side of his constituency! Both men were oblivious that they were being watched, and neither seemed particularly happy with the other. They waved a perfunctory goodbye. As the mayor pulled away, Curtis dallied by his vehicle. Elizabeth made her move.

"Curtis, wait!" Elizabeth yelled as she ran across the street and positioned herself in front of his car door, preventing him from dismissing her.

"Mrs. Evans! Whatever are you doing out here in this weather?" the banker replied incredulously, as the snow peppered down all around them.

"I'm assuming you heard of the break-ins last night," began Elizabeth. "Grace had a very valuable piece of furniture ruined, and if not for a vigilant neighbor, who knows what would have happened at my residence. Curtis, I'm not going to pussyfoot around. Do you have any knowledge of what happened?" Elizabeth genuinely asked.

Hughes looked as if he had just been blindsided and answered rather indignantly. "Absolutely not! Mrs. Evans, I know you are adamantly against the community project and secretly investigating the murder of the author and perhaps even the theft of my mother's jewels. Personally, I think you're asking for trouble. I know nothing of the crimes that have happened of late. I am very sorry you and Mrs. Davis suffered such a terrible fright." Hughes tried to maneuver himself past Elizabeth, but she was having none of it.

"Thank you, Curtis, but do you mind if I ask where you were last night between 5 and 7:30 p.m.?"

"I was at home going over the plans for the community development project, ate a light supper, read a mystery book until 10, and went to bed. And before you ask, no, I do not have an alibi, but that is the truth," answered Curtis, making direct eye contact and sounding exasperated.

"What were you and the mayor discussing just now? He was also seen yesterday talking with James Powell."

"I'm afraid I can't divulge a client's reason for visiting his bank," answered the well reserved banker.

"Who put up the ten thousand dollars to bribe Ollie, Curtis? You, James, or Mayor Beeman? Or perhaps all three of you pitched in?" Curtis refused to speak, so Elizabeth continued. "Why did you insinuate Ollie had taken your underhanded bribe? That was low for even you, Curtis." Elizabeth's words hit hard, drawing another stunned look from Curtis who wasn't used to anyone speaking to him so bluntly, but he held his tongue. "What is so dang intriguing for the three of you to make sure this project goes forward?"

"I am not opening that conversation," answered Hughes.

"I'm also assuming that whoever is pointing the blame at me is also the person who tried to break into my house and put my dog in danger. That lights a fire in my belly, Curtis. I'll find out who did this and why," Elizabeth assured him. "Everyone can count on that."

"I understand, but, again, I had nothing to do with it or know anything about it." Curtis politely scooted her out of the way and opened his car door, abruptly calling their discussion to an end.

Something was nagging at Elizabeth as she crossed the street, so she decided to swing around the block to see if he were still lingering in the parking lot. Although his demeanor suggested some concern for her plight, she intuited he wanted very much for her to leave. Perhaps he was waiting to meet someone he didn't want her to witness. Sure enough, just as Elizabeth was circling back to the bank, an odd red vehicle pulled in next to Hughes, and a brief conversation ensued. The windows were so darkly tinted that it was impossible to identify the driver.

Elizabeth had just placed her hand on the door handle when the unfamiliar car drove swiftly out of the parking lot in the opposite direction with Hughes right on its bumper. By the time Elizabeth got her car reversed, both vehicles had vanished into the evening light, as if they were nothing more than a fleeting vision.

11

More Secrets Revealed

Ana Rees is the only daughter of Owen and Margie Rees. She grew up in a household of four rowdy brothers who gave her nothing but grief. Her father, a struggling alcoholic, is known to be mean as a snake when on a drunken tangent. He always promises he will never touch a drop again once his violence runs out of steam, but that story has been told so many times no one even remotely believes it. Her four brothers seem to follow in dear ole dad's footsteps, apathetic at school and causing havoc in the community. Margie looks twice her age and seems to have given up on any hope of an ordinary, peaceful life. Ana counts the days until she can free herself of a family that is constantly bringing trouble to its doorstep. If Seren Jones

Morgan had known her, she would have said, "Ana's a canary in a crow's nest."

Ana is so different from her parents and siblings, it's hard to believe they share the same DNA. She's as sharp as a tack, has a unique sense of humor that few have ever witnessed, and is as honest as Abe Lincoln himself. Although Ana dresses in Gothic garb, she has no interest in the darker side. She believes her choice of clothing gives her an air of intimidation that keeps bullies and aggressive folks at bay. She has a heart of gold, an empathetic soul, and a quiet demeanor. Ana, unlike her father and brothers, knows that education is the key to successfully hightailing it out of her situation and works very hard at school, earning nothing but *A*'s.

She delights in her involvement with the elderly sisters in their investigation, is vigilant with her assignments from Finch, and secretly craves his praise. She hangs on to his every word and is tingling with anticipation to reveal what she has discovered today, per his private and sophisticated instructions.

Finch quietly entered the village library and found Ana nestled in the ancestry room behind its only computer. "Ana, what have you got for me?"

"Hello, Mr. Finch." She quickly scooted over to make room so he could see the computer screen clearly. "I followed your directions and found something quite interesting, just like you figured I would," she declared, proud as punch. "Is this private enough? The librarian assured me we wouldn't be disturbed."

"Yes, you did well to remain discreet. I'm quite eager to see what you've discovered."

The former federal judge took a seat next to the young, excited genius and stared at her findings. "Oh my word," he whispered.

***

After Finch left the library, he scurried as fast as he could to the parsonage in hopes of catching Pastor White alone. Just as he was approaching the manicured walkway, out stepped the steward. If looks could tell a story, then the pastor's pallid face told a doozy. Rather than speaking, the man of the cloth stood stark still. Once he regained his composure, he motioned for Finch to follow. They entered the cheerful ambience of the foyer as John motioned to an adjoining room containing a comfortable floral print sofa and two leather chairs. The room was painted a soft sage green, and biblical pastoral paintings hung tastefully on each wall. The windows were framed with matching brocade curtains of the same hue and pooled upon a dark wooden floor that looked ancient but well preserved. Each man took a seat before the hearth where a welcoming fire was blazing, making the whole room so relaxing it would be easy to doze off, but not with such pressing issues that faced the two men today.

"Mr. Finch," the nervous reverend began. "What's on your mind?"

"I think you know, John, so I'll let you begin."

"The elderly lady saw me, didn't she?"

"What were you doing there, John? Surely that wasn't you who made an attempt at breaking in and frightening Elizabeth. Her dog was let outside, and she feared it was harmed. If that would have happened, it would have broken her heart. I don't think you're cruel, but I do think you're hiding something. Am I right?"

Pastor White looked down at his hands as if they held the answer, and, therefore, he would have to confess yet again. At last his eyes found a sympathizing face, and he began. "Yes, I was there, but whoever was attempting to break in came awfully close. I interrupted him as he was about to enter. I saw her little dog come out of the house and onto the street. He was causing such a commotion that her neighbor came out and started yelling like David's giant, so I ran. I don't know why I fled. I just wanted to speak to Mrs. Evans. To come clean."

"About the books you mean?"

"Oh, dear lord. You know about that?" Recovering, he continued, "Oh, Mr. Finch, what's happening to me? My world is falling apart. I'm a good person, really I am, but it's those darn books."

As Finch listened patiently, his heart went out to the distraught young man and yearned to turn back time, if only he could.

***

At 4:55 p.m. on the dot, Ollie Williams stepped into the Bibliophile just as Peg was preparing to close up, keys in hand and ready to flip the sign to "Closed."

"Ollie, what a pleasant surprise. What brings you by?" Peg couldn't believe her good luck. It seemed fate had delivered the perfect opportunity for her to question Ollie about the bribe.

"I'm on my way to the children's Christmas meeting, and I heard you had some additional books you were looking to donate. I was told to stop by and pick them up, " Ollie said, patting the snow from his coat.

"The box is in the back. Follow me, and we'll have a cup of hot tea to warm you up."

As the old friends meandered to their favorite niche, Peg pondered how to bring up the delicate topic with her old school chum. "There is something I need to discuss with you," she said, as she poured the tea. Peg took a deep breath and impulsively blurted, "Ollie, you are a dear, dear friend, and I don't like having to broach this subject; however, are you aware that Curtis Hughes and James Powell are insinuating that you may have taken their bribe?"

Ollie, stunned by Peg's bluntness, was grateful to be seated for, otherwise, his knees would have buckled, landing him on the bookstore floor.

Anger crossed his features as he emphatically stated, "I did *not* take a single cent from those rascals!"

"No one thought you did, but I had to ask."

He swallowed hard, his voice barely above a whisper. "I'm scared, Peg. They're threatening me, and I don't know what to do."

"Ollie, what in the world are they threatening with?"

He looked at Peg with such sadness and defeat she was taken aback.

"I have a secret I can't...*won't* reveal...and it's not good."

***

As the street lights began to twinkle, it was obvious to all that the days were getting shorter, and the holidays were imminently close. The small party of seniors tumbled into the Sugar Bowl, eagerly awaiting the feast they were sure Beryl had prepared. They weren't disappointed. A cup of steaming homemade vegetable soup was sitting at each place, ready to warm them up. As they found their seats and began palavering, platters of golden fried chicken, scalloped potatoes, green beans, stewed apples, and piles of buttery biscuits were set before them. A pot of Beryl's famous decaf coffee and a pitcher of decaffeinated iced tea were placed on the table ends, and the friends dug in. As soon as the meal was almost complete, Beryl brought in her award-winning apple pie and a carafe of caramel sauce for easy pouring.

Finch was doing everything he could to hold his excitement in and not rush the ravenous group, but he, too, was about to burst, from food and eager anticipation. He couldn't wait to see their faces, especially Elizabeth's. Hee Haw!

"Well, I was starved, but now I'm about to burst," said Grace between mouthfuls of melt-in-your-mouth pie. "Beryl, this is absolutely delicious!" All the Morgan sisters were excellent cooks, but cooking was a passion for Beryl. Nothing thrilled her more than preparing a sumptuous meal for her family and friends.

Grace glanced up from her dessert, her expression suddenly sober as she looked around the room. Concern etched itself across her features as her eyes dropped to her watch.

"Where's Peg?" quizzed Grace.

"Has anyone seen Peg? She should've been here by now," Beryl said, her voice edged with worry and pained anxiety.

Just then, the door swung open with a loud bang, blown by a ferocious gust of wind. Peg burst in, striding energetically into the diner, breathless and glowing with excitement. Her eyes sparkled, her smile mischievous. "I've got news!"

Everyone stared in stunned silence at Peg's dramatic entrance.

"Ollie stopped by the shop, and I got the scoop!"

"Well, tell us what he said and stop keeping us in suspense," urged Grace.

Peg slipped out of her coat and hung it on the back of her chair, waiting for the group's undivided attention, for she knew what she was about to disclose was a humdinger.

"Ollie, definitely did *not* accept one red cent from those scoundrels...and guess what...." She paused for effect.

"Spit it out!" Grace said impatiently.

"Ollie has an awful secret." Peg looked around the table to gage their reactions.

"What! What is it?" asked Elizabeth, irritated at her sister for stringing them along instead of just telling them the juicy news.

"I don't know. He didn't say what his secret was, and he refused to reveal it. But, I was dying to ask. James and Curtis are threatening to expose it if he doesn't vote for the project. That must've been what they were discussing when Elizabeth saw them all waving their arms in the park."

"I just can't image what kind of dark secret sweet Ollie would have that would terrify him like that," mused Elizabeth.

"Well, whatever it is, he's as twitchy as a squirrel on espresso that it's going to come out."

Grace remained stoic as a mouse, for she knew exactly what that secret was.

"Good job, Peg. That was excellent intel," praised Finch to a beaming Peg. "Now if there's nothing else…"

"I don't want anyone to be angry with me, but I went to see Curtis Hughes today," blurted Elizabeth.

"You didn't," said Beryl, looking thoroughly disgusted. "After I told you not to."

Elizabeth held her hands up as if surrendering and said, "Hear me out." She proceeded to retell her observations of the mayor coming out of the bank with Curtis after closing hours, a detailed summary of her conversation with Hughes, and the strange car event.

"I think our beloved mayor is involved with our chief suspects in some profitable, and possibly shady, dealings. They're up to something, and we have to find out what's going on to either nail them or eliminate them as suspects," stated Elizabeth.

"I agree with Elizabeth," replied Grace. "So we need a specific plan to get answers."

"Agreed," chorused Beryl and Peg.

"Elizabeth, please do not put yourself in any more danger. You did discover some interesting pieces to add to our puzzle, but you must agree that if you are to do any more private sleuthing, you must take one of us with you and let the rest of us know where and with whom you're meeting. Do you agree? We also must have a backup plan so we are all informed beforehand to keep us all safe, *especially* Elizabeth and Grace," proposed Finch.

"He's right," chimed in Beryl. You and Grace have both been victimized, and you could have easily lost your dog, and you're lucky you didn't. I second Finch's suggestion."

"Agreed," responded Grace and Peg.

I know one thing, thought Grace, when something happens to that dog, I'm leaving town. She'd seen Elizabeth's heart broken before, and the way she loved that animal, well, Grace just couldn't stand to watch her sister fall into such utter grief again.

"Oh, all right. I won't go against all of you," said Elizabeth, who was disgruntled and unhappy with the compromise. Elizabeth had a stubborn streak that often got her into trouble with her dogged attitude.

Ana remained silent for not wanting to interfere with family issues. She had dealt with enough of those with her own kin. However, she was literally vibrating with fevered exhilaration at the information she and Finch had in store for them.

"Now that this is agreed upon, let's move on to what Ana has uncovered for us," said Finch with almost as much anticipation as his protege.

"Go ahead, sir. I think you should be the one to tell them," Ana suggested.

Sir? thought Elizabeth. This is getting thick. They must have found something very interesting the way they're acting.

"Ana gets all the credit. She found the link to Pastor John White and Virginia Pierce. I spoke with John earlier today, and he confirmed what Ana discovered."

"Oh, get on with it. I'm about to explode!" exclaimed Peg.

"Virginia Pierce is a fraud," said Finch so pompously Elizabeth thought she would gag. "She is John White's..."

"Lover!" interjected Peg. "I could tell by the way they acted. Yep, no doubt about it."

"Actually, their relationship is quite platonic." Peg's face fell in utter disappointment. "Virginia and John are first cousins and have a secret pact. John writes naughty romance novels, and Virginia publishes them as her own, using a pseudonym. They split the very lucrative profits. That's how she and her husband Ed could afford the down payment on the inn. They followed John here because she wants to keep the pressure on him to continue writing the racy novels so they can keep the Holly Hill afloat. John, on the other hand, was desperate to keep Virginia out of jail with her thieving habits for fear they would be exposed, and he would lose his parish. That's why he devised that ridiculous scheme about finding Elizabeth's scarf on the town hall floor. The poor man is about to come unhinged," concluded Finch.

"Boy, that's a jaw dropper! I sure didn't see that coming. I almost feel sorry for him," opined Peg.

"Oh, for goodness' sake," berated Beryl. "He's a man of the cloth and profiting from smutty books. What's this world coming to?"

"What's Virginia's pseudonym?" wondered Peg out loud.

"Magnolia Hawthorn," replied Ana, as Finch was looking through his notes to locate the pen name.

Oh, thought Peg, who looked a little sheepish, for she had read every one of Magnolia Hawthorn's books and enjoyed them immensely.

"Wait a minute! What did he say about breaking into my house?" pursued Elizabeth.

"Oh, yes!" He almost added he was so excited about the book news that he totally forgot about the break-in but knew Elizabeth would have some kind of senile retort, so he refrained. "He was at Elizabeth's house the night of the robbery. He actually came upon the perpetrator in just the nick of time and scared him off. He then saw Mrs. Edwards come out of her house to see what the ruckus was all about, and...he ran. Poor chap. He feels everything is his life is unravelling."

"But what did he want with me?" Elizabeth's left eyebrow went up as though she wasn't buying White's scared little boy scenario.

"He came to apologize to you in person about the scarf fiasco. I personally thought that was quite big of him."

"So I guess we can eliminate them as suspects." Elizabeth blew out an exaggerated breath and was a bit disappointed, yet fascinated that North Falls was home to an actual bestselling author, even if by questionable means.

"Yes, John is adamant that neither he nor Ed and Virginia know anything about our murder victim. So, let's move on to the next bit of captivating information about none other than Marshall Wymark himself," boasted Finch, proud as a peacock. "Ana, would you please reveal your riveting findings on Wymark?"

This man should have been a ringmaster, thought Elizabeth. He could make a pigeon sound interesting.

"Of course, Mr. Finch. Marshall Wymark, as I said before, does not exist, at least not by that name, but he does exist by another: Richard Gerald Bartholomew. He's British."

"British? But he didn't talk with an accent," said Grace, who spent more time conversing with him than the others.

"That may be true, but he is definitely British. Richard Bartholomew, aka Wymark, is a member of Scotland Yard dealing with the Arts and Crafts Movement. He investigates thefts that originally were committed in England but have crossed the Atlantic to avoid prosecution in the British Isles. It seems our murder victim was investigating a crime that somehow involves North Falls."

"If I may elaborate, a crime was committed *in* Europe, but the thief has invaded our innocent little community. Bartholomew was sent here to investigate," postulated Finch.

Elizabeth was captivated but kept her interest hidden for fear of stroking Finch's already inflated ego.

"You mean that there *is* an international thief among us?" Grace couldn't fathom it.

"Well, what do you know! Cora was right! I can't believe it," exclaimed Elizabeth. Cora, co-owner of the cross-stitch shop, had confided in Elizabeth that she believed there was an international jewel thief in their midst, referring to Curtis Hughes's deceased mother's stolen jewels. Elizabeth told the group about Cora's assessment.

"Well, let's be clear. We don't know if the Hughes robbery has anything to do with Mr. Bartholomew's investigation," interjected Finch.

"This is so hard to believe," bemoaned Beryl, who was becoming more and more discouraged at the reality of old-fashioned decency's decline.

"So, how in the world did Bartholomew come to suspect that someone in North Falls was involved in a European heist," wondered Elizabeth, "and could this crime in any way be linked to the community project?"

"We have no proof yet, but this case just keeps getting more interesting," replied Finch, and with that, he adjourned the meeting.

***

"Christmas is bearing down on us as this investigation just gets more complicated," mused Peg as they all meandered home through the picturesque streets, leaving footprints in their wake. Peg bid them good night as she turned onto her welcoming tree-lined street, now bare except for nature's glistening frosting, and where her beloved Jack was waiting.

"By the way," asked Grace, "when are you expecting my nieces to come home? I miss those girls."

"They're flying home in the next couple of days so we can enjoy some holiday time before the big day. I hope nothing comes up at work to delay them. I miss them so much," smiled Elizabeth.

As they stopped in front of Grace's residence, Finch asked meekly, "Do you suppose I'll get to meet them?"

"I suppose you'll see them about. They love their hometown." Turning her attention to Grace, she artfully changed the subject. "Night, Grace. Would you like us to go in and check your house before we go?"

"No, I'll be fine. Call me when you get settled in so I don't worry," replied Grace. She loved and fretted about her youngest sibling, even though she put on a tough facade. Elizabeth had such a heartache with Sam, her ex-husband, and Grace knew the wound was still deeply raw.

"See you tomorrow," called Elizabeth, as she and Finch slowly zigzagged through the mounting snow. As they rounded the corner to Elizabeth's home, she heard Abner greeting her with his hound-dog wail.

"No wonder your neighbor heard that! Lucky for you," said Finch.

"Yep, he's quite the watchdog."

"Do you want me to check your house before you go in? I don't mind," offered Finch.

"Oh no, thank you. I'm a big girl. I'm sure I'm much scarier than you."

"Night then. Oh, and you may be right," Finch added with a flirtatious wink.

"Right? Right about what?"

"Being scary," he rebuffed. As he turned, she could just make out a parting smirk.

As she closed the door, her little pal was wiggling from snout to tail. What a joy it is to have your dog always happy to see you!

Once Elizabeth and Abner were tucked snugly into bed, which had become a nightly ritual since the break-in, her thoughts turned to her daughters, whom she missed with a deep ache. She began planning a mental holiday list of excursions and events they could do during their stay. They always enjoyed the carol walk and sipping hot chocolate with friends at the end of the evening. Oh, she thought, we'll get some really exquisite paper, ribbons, and bows and wrap everything early so we can watch holiday movies and all the Harry Potter videos. The girls love watching Harry Potter movies at Christmas. And the baking! We'll try something different this year. Just as Elizabeth was about to fall into slumber, her train of thought took a U-turn and began to trace the events since the loss of her scarf. All at once, she sat straight up in bed and said, "We never found out what Curtis and James were arguing about at the gala!" I'll have to remember to bring that up next time, she thought. And with that, she lay back, as visions of sugar plums danced in her head.

12

More Trouble

It was another overcast day, making the weatherman appear to be a gifted prognosticator as snow threatened yet again. Ice was forecasted for the early morning hours, and a warning was issued that much of the state could possibly be without electricity. "Bundle up if you have to go out. Otherwise, stay inside," admonished the state patrol. "It will be dangerous traveling if only to the grocery store."

Finch was furiously making his way to the Cupboard. He had just left Officer Ruff's office on what he hoped the good lawman believed was a goodwill mission to update him on the news he was allegedly hearing at the grocery. Officer Ruff, who followed the letter of the law, had absolutely no news concerning an open case that he was willing to trade for Finch's good-citizen report.

Dang it, that man is no help whatsoever, thought the former judge. Then he had a thought, a most reckless thought. Do I dare? he pondered. He then made his final decision. Finch took out his cell phone and made a call. No going back now.

***

As the amateur sleuths made their way to the Sugar Bowl after closing hours, Beryl was ready for them with another tantalizing meal of meat loaf, baked beans, creamy mashed potatoes, coleslaw, crescent rolls, and warm homemade chocolate pudding, topped with fresh heavy cream. Finch had called her earlier and told her about the urgent meeting. Between the two of them, they contacted the entire group, who was excited about another interesting new development.

"Due to the incoming inclement weather, I think it best we have our meeting while enjoying our supper. Are you all okay with that?" asked Finch, who looked as if he were about to burst, and not from the hefty meal he was yet to consume.

After everyone present agreed, Finch began by clearing his throat.

Oh, good grief. He's milking this for all it's worth. This better be good, thought Elizabeth as she inwardly groaned.

"Earlier this morning, I did my second update with our illustrious police force. Officer Ruff still refuses to give me any pertinent information concerning our case, *but* I did discover something of profound interest." Finch took a deep breath.

"Oh, come on, tell us and quit stalling," pleaded Peg.

"Mr. Bartholomew, aka Wymark, was *not* killed by Elizabeth's holiday scarf." Everyone stopped eating and sat as quietly as church mice, forks suspended in mid-air. "Bartholomew was given a deadly injection of a fast acting drug," emphasized Finch. "Then whoever killed him put him in a Santa suit and tied the scarf around his neck. Therefore, Elizabeth's scarf was *not* the murder weapon as we all believed, but simply an added touch to a very sordid deed, completed after his death," finished Finch. His theatrics were first rate.

The air was so thick it could have been cut with a knife. The aging group was struck dumb. Finally, Grace found her voice. "Then, there must be more than one killer."

"Absolutely," agreed Beryl. "There is no way anyone could accomplish such a feat all on his own. He had to have had help." Beryl was incredibly intelligent and could piece together information quickly and accurately.

"This puts a whole new spin on the murder. Who would be so brazen as to drug someone, take the time to dress him in a Santa suit, tie *my* scarf around his neck, and then move the body outside in the snow, just as partygoers are exiting the inn?" Elizabeth pondered, flabbergasted by this new revelation.

"Someone definitely not afraid of getting caught; that's for sure," said Grace ruminating. "But, why would anyone want to demean a human being in that way, just for show? That's psychotic and gives me the willies."

And then Beryl understood where the confidential information came from. "Ana, did you hack into Officer Ruff's police files to read the autopsy report?" she asked warily.

"I did," answered Ana, without hesitation.

"Impressive," said Grace.

Elizabeth turned and looked Finch squarely in the eye. He knew his decision to involve Ana with his latest request would raise her hackles. He braced himself for an old-fashioned tongue-lashing.

"What? Are you insane? Asking this child to do the dirty work again! What happens if she gets caught? What happens if we get caught?" Elizabeth was livid.

"Oh no, Mrs. Evans. That will never happen," replied Ana so self-assuredly that the entire group was flabbergasted. Here was meek little Ana speaking up with such confidence they couldn't quite believe this was the same shy, awkward girl who sunk so far into herself only a short time ago. Whatever effect this investigation was having on her was undoubtedly a positive one. "As I told you before," she continued, "I am very good at what I do. They'll never trace it to me."

"How can you be so sure? You're not the only computer expert out there. What if they bring in a specialist?" Elizabeth asked.

"Don't worry. I covered myself. I always do," replied Ana calmly with a smile that spoke volumes.

"She's not worried, you shouldn't be worried. Trust us," Finch spoke softly.

"What choice do any of us have at this point?" Elizabeth sighed, exasperated. "It's time I went home anyway. The weather's getting pretty hazardous." Then she whispered with a bit of glee, clearly trying to lighten the mood. "I wouldn't want Beryl to worry I may fall and bruise my bum!"

"Wait a minute, Elizabeth. We need to discuss this a bit more. Does anyone have any idea why Elizabeth and Grace have been targeted? They must pose a threat somehow," said Peg.

"Or we're the scapegoats to divert attention away from the scumbag, whoever he is, onto us. Elizabeth's scarf may not be the murder weapon, but someone wanted it to look as if Elizabeth were the murderer; otherwise, why use her scarf?" Grace reasoned.

"Let's all think about this and reconvene when the weather permits. We can always have a conference call if need be," said Finch. "The snow is accumulating rather quickly."

"One more thing, I almost forgot." Elizabeth quickly continued in case Finch decided to make an unnecessary jab about her memory. "Grace and Peg, remember the night of the gala when Curtis and James got into a heated confrontation and spilled the champagne?"

"Yes, that's right," said Grace.

"We thought they were going to knock each other out then and there," recalled Peg. "I wonder what that was all about?"

"Somehow, we all forgot about it. We need to find out what they were so worked up about. I'm sure it's crucial to the case," finished Elizabeth.

"Good job, Elizabeth. I forgot about that, too. No wonder with all the excitement going on," added Grace.

"Finch, why don't you question the boys this time? Grace and Elizabeth need to stay away from them. At least for now," pleaded Beryl.

"Of course. We'd best get going. Thank you again, Beryl, for the wonderful meal."

Beryl and her sisters quickly packed any remaining food for hungry husbands and midnight snackers, and out the door they went. It was snowing like the dickens, and the going was slow. The sisters filled the judge in on what he had missed at the inn's holiday party and discussed what possible cause could have been the subject of the caustic disagreement between Curtis and James. Finch promised to talk with each gentleman to see if either were willing to divulge any information. It would be a moot plan. One of the suspects would soon become victim number two.

***

Later that night in the swanky part of town, one of its residents was awakened by a disturbing noise. He quietly left the comfort of his palatial bed, listening intently for another peculiar sound. He cautiously descended the magnificent staircase. Pellets of ice were pummeling the large glass windows and elegant French doors. No doubt the electricity would soon succumb to the heavy weight of the frozen lines. The patio lights flickered and went out. Something was off. He felt it and was stung with fear. His heart began racing, and he was struggling to breathe normally. Why didn't I think to bring a flashlight? he admonished himself. He felt a presence in the house. Impossible, he reminded himself. He had top-of-the-line security. As the lights blinked and struggled for survival, he could just make out a human figure seated, of all places, at the grand piano. "Who are you?" he asked, trying to sound in control, but his voice betrayed him.

The intruder patted the bench for the homeowner to sit. As the outside light flared again, he then recognized a familiar face.

"What the devil are you doing here? It's the middle of the night." The homeowner was terrified but tried to sound annoyed. "How did you get in?" he stammered.

The figure remained silent, making the macabre scene more freakish.

"Look, I told you, I won't say anything if you just return the jewels. Please leave."

Once again, the intruder beckoned him to the bench. As the gentleman stood his ground, baffled at the unwanted presence, his mind was sending an alarm. The intruder slowly rose. Before the master of the house could react, he felt a violent stab on the right side of his neck and slid slowly to the floor. A second figure rounded on him to help lessen the fall for fear of being heard. The victim tried to speak, but it was futile. The two assailants stood over him until he fell into a lasting state of unconsciousness, and then they did the deed.

***

Blodwyn Powell was sound asleep when an odd sense of dread awakened her. She looked at the clock and was startled that it read 2:35 a.m. She turned to rouse her husband but was alarmed he was missing. Thoughts began to swirl in her head. Could he be ill? Perhaps he fell, and that was what woke her? Was there an intruder? That's nonsense, she told herself. The alarm would have gone off. Where in the world was James? She was frightened. Slowly, she left the cozy warmth of the bed and put on her robe and slippers. Although the house was warm, there was a definite chill in the air. As she approached the stairs, her fear intensified. She hit the light switch, but nothing happened. She returned to the bedroom, extracted a candle from the nightstand, and lit it. A mellow glow guided her way. I'm going to give him a piece of my mind for scaring me like this, she told herself. It was at this point that she noticed the French doors were slightly ajar. That's strange, she thought. Just then, the outside lights quivered, and the house was cast in murky twilight. Just as quickly, the lights were once again extinguished. "James? Where are you?" No answer came. Blodwyn tried the light switch at the bottom of the stairs, but no reassuring illumination rescued her from the searing darkness. "James, I'm frightened. Are you down here? Answer me, please." Silence permeated throughout the house. "James, if you don't answer me, I'm going to call the police." When she received no response, she quickly retrieved her cell phone, delighted she had service. She was immediately connected to the station. "This is Blodwyn Powell on Sycamore Circle. I can't find my husband. I think someone may have tried to break in." The lights flickered, fighting for life, but were soon extinguished once again, but not before Blodwyn got a glimpse of a strange mound beyond the patio. "Dear God," she murmured into the phone. I think there's a homeless person in my backyard!"

***

Elizabeth's phone rang at 8 o'clock sharp. It was Finch.

"Elizabeth, we're meeting at the Sugar Bowl now. There's been a development."

"What kind of a development?"

"Just get over there as soon as you can and be careful. It's treacherous out there."

"Finch, you're scaring me. Is everyone alright?"

"Your sisters are fine and are congregating as we speak. I'll see you there." The line went dead.

***

The streets were still covered, but clearing was underway. The weather decided to hesitate before delivering more damage. Fortunately, the electricity was restored, and businesses opened one by one. The small party of amateur sleuths sat in the Sugar Bowl's backroom waiting for Finch and Ana to arrive with the mysterious development. Beryl brought out freshly baked turnovers of all varieties and piping hot coffee.

Ana and Finch could be heard stomping their feet to relieve their boots of an overload of snow. As they took off their coats and hats, they made their way to the table, where anxious faces awaited more bad news.

"Good morning, everyone. I'm glad you all made it in safely. We've learned some disturbing news. Let's grab a cup of coffee and a pastry, and we'll begin," said Finch. The group couldn't read Finch's expression, but they knew it had to be something pretty big to drag them out in such severe weather.

"As you know, Ana monitors police reports, scanners, emergency calls, and...so forth. A little before three this morning, there was a call made from the Powell residence. Mrs. Powell reported she couldn't locate her husband and was in a panic. In the midst of the call, she thought a homeless person had wandered into her backyard and collapsed in the snow. The police and ambulance arrived shortly thereafter. However, it was not a homeless person. It was James Powell. Nothing could be done. He was already dead," Finch finished solemnly.

"Dead? What happened?" asked Peg, astounded by the grisly news.

"Actually, I'm afraid to guess," responded Beryl. "I fear this isn't all you have to tell us. Am I right?"

"What could be worse?" added Grace. "Is there more?"

Oh, for goodness' sake, thought Elizabeth. He's in the height of his glory, holding us in suspense and stringing us along for theatrics. Will the man never cease? A man has been killed.

"There is something very alarming about Mr. Powell's death," Finch paused for effect.

"He was found..."

"He was found what?" prompted Peg, her tolerance waned by the unnecessary drawn-out melodrama.

"He was found wearing a Santa suit."

***

Once the group processed the disconcerting news, everyone was speaking at once, trying to decipher precisely what had happened.

"James had to have seen or heard something that put him into danger," began Peg. "Oh, this is just terrible." All those present were undeniably distraught.

"It had to have something to do with the mall project," announced Grace.

"Or the stolen jewelry. Let's not forget about that," reminded Beryl.

Elizabeth, Finch, and Ana remained deep in thought. One could practically see their minds at work.

"What do you think, Ana?" Grace asked.

After a moment of thought, she spoke. "Someone close to Mr. Powell had to be responsible. How else could they have gotten into his house? According to police records, the Powells have state-of-the-art security. I'm assuming that Mr. Powell told someone what he discovered, and whatever that something was put him in grave danger."

"I think you're absolutely right, Ana. Now, we need to figure out whom he confided in and what it was that targeted him to be the next victim," contemplated Beryl.

"For starters, we need Ana to dig into the cause of death, so we'll need a peek at the autopsy report," Finch said pompously.

Elizabeth shot him a sharp look, clearly annoyed by how casually he kept dragging Ana into things.

"I'm not a betting man," he continued, "but I think it would be a good wager that the murders were done exactly the same, right down to the Santa suit," added Finch, careful not to make eye contact with the North Falls' disciplinarian.

"Wait a minute," interrupted Peg. "Let me make sure I got this right. Someone James allegedly knew broke into his house undetected in the middle of a snowstorm by disengaging the security system, killed him, dressed him in a Santa suit, and somehow got him outside to be discovered by his wife in his own backyard?"

"That's it in a nutshell," confirmed Beryl.

"Which reinforces our earlier assumptions. This was premeditated, and there must be more than one perpetrator," stated Grace.

"Wow, so much to take in. I think I'll take a walk and get my thoughts in order, if we're finished here," said Elizabeth, visibly upset at the turn of events.

As Elizabeth gathered her things, Grace joined her. "I'm coming with you. I could use some fresh air, too."

And then, right on cue: "Be careful out there, girls. It's still slippery as the dickens. You don't want to fall and break a hip," called Beryl, as Elizabeth and Grace exchanged amused glances and stifled smiles.

"The snowplows have been out, and the sidewalks have been heavily salted. We'll be fine," countered Grace.

With no destination in mind, they turned south, toward Powell's office. The little business sat near the end of Main Street. Holiday decorations accented the front door, and a Merry Christmas sign stood by the walkway. Just as the two sisters neared the establishment, Elizabeth grabbed Grace's arm and pulled her into the doorway of the Wooly Lamb, a clothing store specializing in wool garments and accessories for the home.

"What's the matter?" Grace asked, startled.

"Do you see that car parked behind Powell's office?"

"Yes, what about it?"

"That's the vehicle I saw that day at the bank. I thought Curtis acted as if he were trying to get rid of me when I was questioning him about his conversation with the mayor. That very car pulled up, and Curtis followed it. I tried to follow them, but I wasn't fast enough. I need to get into that office and find out who's driving that car. Wait here."

"Oh, no you don't. Not by yourself," said Grace. "Didn't we all agree to work in pairs? I'll go in and flush out whoever it is, and you wait by the car. Copy down the license plate number, and, if we're lucky, we may be able to corner them and ask a few questions. Oh boy, Beryl's gonna have a fit," Grace muttered, blowing out a breath of sibling fear at the tongue-lashing she and Elizabeth were sure to get.

They dashed crossed the street, coats and colorful scarves flapping in the wind. It might have been a comical scene, as they slipped and skidded across the frozen street, if not for the urgency that was driving them. Grace disappeared inside, while Elizabeth crept cautiously around the building, rummaging in her purse for a pen and paper. She stumbled and dropped her notebook in the frozen mess, just as the driver emerged from the rear of the office door. Before she had time to react, the unidentified person of interest was already in the car, haphazardly speeding away.

Seconds later, Grace came around the side of the building, looking bewildered. "Where'd they go?"

"Whoever it was took off like a mad bull. The windows are so tinted it's impossible to see inside that dang car. I'm sure those are way too dark to be legal," panted Elizabeth, her voice tinged with disappointment. "Did you see who it was before they came out the back door?"

"No, as soon as I went in, I heard the door slam. Loud. If I didn't know better, I'd say they were arguing. The receptionist said she didn't know the woman's name. She played the grieving routine perfectly. Like she was too upset about James to talk. Rubbish!" scoffed Grace. "Did you get a good enough look?"

"Yes and no," said Elizabeth slowly.

"What do you mean 'yes and no'?" Grace asked, looking perplexed.

"It means I think we need to talk to the mayor."

13

An Informative Chat

After Elizabeth filled Grace in on what she suspected, their next stop was the mayor's home. Unfortunately, neither the mayor nor his wife, Mary Beeman, answered the door, and the distinctive car was not in the driveway.

"Next stop, town hall. If Tom's not home, then he's got to be in his office," announced Elizabeth. They did indeed find Mayor Beeman behind his desk, looking for all the world like a hardworking public servant. "Good morning, Tom. Could we steal some of your busy time for a quick chat?" smiled Grace. No one in North Falls could turn down Grace and that charm of hers.

"Of course, ladies. What can I do for you?" The mayor stood, all smiles. "Please have a seat. What brings you to town hall today in this nasty weather?"

The ladies took the offered chairs, and Grace spoke first. "Would you tell us what you were really doing in Mr. Powell's office the day I saw you there?"

Mayor Beeman was taken aback at the abruptness of the question and appeared quite uncomfortable. "Oh, as I told you before, Mary and I are looking for another place."

"We think we may have seen your wife at Powell's office earlier. I'm sure you heard about poor James," Grace said sadly.

"Yes, that was quite a shock."

"She left before we could get a word," said Elizabeth. "We tried catching her at home, but she wasn't there. Any idea where she might be?"

"I have no idea. Why do you want to speak with Mary?" questioned the mayor guardedly.

"I'm going to be honest with you, Tom. We're quietly investigating the murder of Mr. Wymark. You know that Elizabeth's scarf was found wrapped around the dead man's neck. Then someone came in the delivery entrance to my shop and scribbled a warning on the surface of a costly piece of furniture and ruined it. That very same evening, someone attempted to break into

Elizabeth's house and left the exact same warning. Her poor dog was let outside in the weather, running the streets, and could have been hit. Who knows what would have happened if she were at home? Someone seems to be pointing the finger at Elizabeth and warning us to stay away from the investigation." Then Grace leaned in and, with a spark of steel in her voice, said, "That makes us very determined."

"We believe it has to do with our being against the community project," said Elizabeth. "I saw James, Curtis Hughes, and Ollie Williams arguing in the park the day after the town meeting. Ollie said Curtis and James offered him some big money to change his mind and endorse the project, which of course he declined. Everything that has happened seems to revert back to that darn complex."

"But what's that got to do with Mary? I'm confused," said the mayor, trying hard to connect the dots and hoping they weren't treading down a dangerous path.

"I was waiting to talk with Curtis Hughes when I saw you and him come out of the bank after hours. Mind if I ask what you were discussing?" asked Elizabeth, growing excited and ignoring the topic of his wife as she watched him twitch.

"Why would you want to know about that, Elizabeth? It was nothing really," he answered as if he couldn't quite catch his breath.

"Then would you care to tell me? I'm not on the best of terms with Curtis, and I've been trying to discover who tried to break into my home."

"You think Curtis had something to do with that?" The mayor appeared more rattled and began to squirm. "Listen, he called and asked if I would meet with him a few minutes before the bank closed so we could talk privately. Said he had something important to talk with me about. I went to hear what he had to say. I was curious. That's all."

"So what did he want to tell you? Please, Tom, this is important," implored Elizabeth.

"He asked if I would support that dang mall. That whole ordeal has been nothing but a headache and a noose around my neck. I keep telling him as mayor I have to listen to my constituency. There are too many against it, so I told him it's not the right time. He gave me this big community spiel, and I told him I would think about it. That's was it," finished the politician.

"Did he offer you any financial promises as he did Ollie Williams?" asked Grace brazenly.

"Absolutely not!" puffed the mayor. "I am a man of high ethical and moral standards and take my office seriously. I would never take a bribe."

"Does your wife Mary drive a red sports car? It's just I've never seen one like that before," acknowledged Elizabeth, switching up the conversation to keep him unaware of where the discussion was headed.

"Yes, that's one of them European cars, an Alfa Romeo 33 Stradale. That car can kick up its heels, let me tell you! I don't know why she insisted on buying it." The mayor appeared embarrassed. "I told her as a local politician, I don't think voters would take too kindly for their mayor's wife to be riding around in an expensive foreign sports car. I prefer American made myself." He sat up a bit straighter, pulled on his lapels, and smiled as if he were the paragon of patriotism.

Elizabeth tried oh so hard not to roll her eyes or stick her finger down her throat but continued the thread she was weaving. "The reason I'm asking is that after you left that evening, Curtis stayed in the parking lot as if he were waiting for someone. Then I saw that car pull alongside him. After what appeared to be a brief conversation, the car drove off pretty fast with Curtis right behind it. I'll be honest. I tried to follow them, but by the time I got turned around, they were nowhere to be seen. Do you have any idea why Mary would be meeting with Curtis after hours?" Elizabeth was on to something. She could feel it in her gut and wanted to keep the conversation flowing.

"You saw Mary talking with Curtis? Are you sure?"

"I couldn't see who was driving because of the darkly tinted windows, but if that's her car, who else could it have been? Let's face it. That car is easy to identify."

"I have no idea what she was doing there, but I will definitely ask her about it. I'm sure it's nothing."

"Does Mary know that James was killed early this morning?" asked Grace, confident the entire village would be abuzz with the alarming news.

"Yes," the mayor slowly replied. "Why?"

"Well, I was wondering why she would stop at his office if she knew he obviously wouldn't be in?" Grace smoothly asked.

"She was probably consoling her niece after what happened to poor ole James. Tragic wasn't it? Just like that guy up at the inn."

"Wait a minute. Maggie is your wife's niece?" Grace asked incredulously.

"Hold on. Who's Maggie?" interrupted Elizabeth.

"Maggie is, or was, James's receptionist. I met her when I first questioned James about the meeting in the park that you witnessed."

"I wonder why I've never met her?" Elizabeth mused, puzzled at the thought of someone new moving to North Falls, without her hearing the first thing about it.

"That's because she's been living in London," boasted Beeman. "She went to a private school there when Morris, that's their father, was transferred years ago. You remember Morris, don't you? He was married to Mary's sister Monica."

"I do, but goodness, that's been a while," said Grace, trying to remember exactly when was the last time she saw Morris Dolman.

"Poor Monica was heartbroken after the divorce and moved back to the states. The girls refused to come with their mother, and because they were of age, she couldn't force them. They recently decided to move back to North Falls, and Mary is absolutely thrilled," replied the mayor happily.

"Hold on. Girls? You mean Maggie has a sister?"

"Yes, that would be Macie. She's pretty quiet and not real friendly." His lip curled in a funny movement that couldn't disguise his unfavorable opinion. "She kind of keeps to herself, but, boy, is she smart! She works up at the inn. She was devastated when that guy was murdered up there. What was his name again?"

"Marshall Wymark. Did she know him?" scrutinized Grace.

"No, I wouldn't think so. The girls haven't been here that long."

"I've met her." She was the maid who warned her about Virginia Pierce's foul mood. "Was she working the night of the murder?" Elizabeth was now riveted to her seat.

"Oh yes, poor thing," the mayor said, looking distressed. "She was quite traumatized by the whole thing. We had the awfullest time persuading her to go back to work for fear she might get fired. Mary told her it may be difficult to find another position in a town this size. She wasn't the least bit happy about it, but she bit the bullet in the end and went back." The mayor leaned forward and whispered conspiratorially as if he were entrusting them with a grave family secret. "Just between us, she hates that job. She says Virginia's hard to please and acts all uppity. I think Macie, with all that European education, is a bit snooty herself and feels being a maid is beneath her. By any chance, you don't have any openings, do you, Grace?" he asked hopefully.

"No, I'm afraid I don't. I was lucky to find Ivy Campbell. She's been a treasure."

"Well, we've taken up enough of your time. We should be going," said Elizabeth, bubbling with excitement and itching to leave so she could relay the news she and Grace had uncovered to her comrades.

"Let us know what you find out from Mary, and if you think of anything else, please let us know," said Grace, as the sisters rose to leave.

"As mayor, I want to serve all the people. We need to solve our problems and help each other out. It's all about building a community. It's the way we do things here in North Falls. Merry Christmas, ladies, and thanks for stopping by."

Tom Beeman may have put on a jolly face, but he was shaken, terrified that if those nosy women found out the real reason Curtis and James were at odds with each other, his wife would kill him. And if Elizabeth Evans found out he lied, well, she'd probably do the same.

***

As the Morgan sisters exited the town hall, Grace snickered. "Elizabeth, you were absolutely brilliant in there! You discovered Maggie has a sister, the girls lived in Europe, Macie was working the night of the murder, Mary owns the mysterious car *and* is their aunt, plus Curtis is still trying to get that project passed!"

"I have a sinking feeling there's more to come. But have you ever heard a more rousing re-election speech? Good thing for us he's running next year. He may not have been quite so forthcoming." Yet the Morgan sisters had no way of knowing that the mayor purposefully withheld a very important piece of the puzzle that would reveal the very reason for the altercation between Curtis and James the night of the party. But then again, his wife would, indeed, kill him.

***

As the sisters marched down the snowy street, they were as giddy as two schoolgirls with their newfound information. Elizabeth couldn't wait to see Finch's face when she announced what they had discovered. Grace had just gotten off the phone with him to gather everyone at the diner, when Elizabeth's phone sang out a cheery jingle. As she answered the call, her buoyant mood was immediately dissipated. It was not the merry message she was anticipating.

IRIS WARDLOW

14

I Love My Nieces To Pieces

Mary was the older of the two Miller sisters. Monica and she grew up in a modest two-story home with a spacious front lawn on Ferguson Street, a quiet tree-lined lane near the outskirts of town. Monica was always more talented, more beautiful, more popular, and more intelligent. She could read her assignments quickly and efficiently, and her comprehension was through the roof. One would think she had a photographic memory. She could waltz through fifty math problems each night and still have plenty of time to watch her favorite TV shows, ride her bike, or read a Nancy Drew mystery. Mary, on the other hand, struggled with many of her academic subjects and needed additional help from her parents in the evening, who were not happy to oblige. They would say such things as, "I'm too tired," or "It's been too long since I've been in school." But the comment that stung the most was, "Can't you ask Monica for help? I know she hasn't had your subjects yet, but I bet she could figure them out." This only increased Mary's insecurity and anger at her younger sibling's far-reaching abilities. Monica this and Monica that. She was the golden girl, and Mary was always scrambling to catch a crumb of her parents' praise.

Although Mary wasn't as eye-catching, she was liked by her peers and tried to be polite and personable. So when Monica and the influential and wealthy Morris Dolman divorced, it was now time for Mary to shine as the first lady of North Falls. Who's more successful now? She tried not to gloat, but after decades of living in the shadow of her younger sister, she was ready to strut her stuff. Too bad her parents hadn't lived to see the fall of Monica Miller Dolman and the rise of Mary Miller Beeman.

Mary enjoyed the status her husband's position as mayor gave her in the community. People looked up to them as leaders in the village. She was happy in North Falls, where the days were predictable, and the faces familiar. Tom was indeed upset when she purchased the Alfa Romeo, but it was mainly done to impress her nieces, who had returned from England. She even let Maggie borrow it from time to time.

Maggie Dolman was as alluring and fashion savvy as her jet-setting mother, but it was Macie who emerged as the natural leader, a young woman with a wildly creative imagination and an unshakable sense of authority. She had a knack for bending individuals to her way of thinking and seldom failed in getting the results she diligently pursued. Although she wasn't the type to turn heads, she was a very attractive young woman. Her stylish short cut of tawny hair framed sharp and penetrating brown eyes. She had a good figure, though she preferred clothing that blended in rather than stood out, one of the reasons she hated the frilly Victorian getup she was forced to wear at the inn.

The Dolman sisters had led privileged lives, going to private schools, attaining college degrees from Oxford, gallivanting across Europe, and attending prestigious social events. Then, out of nowhere, with no warning, they show up in North Falls, crashing the holidays with her and Tom! So yes, she bought the car so her hoity-toity nieces could see that she and Tom were thought of as important pillars in the community. Competing with Monica's lifestyle had always been challenging, but it was impossible to ignore just how much better off she was now compared to her sad, depressed, and divorced sibling.

Mary, for reasons she didn't fully understand, felt surprising sympathy for these affluent young women. She believed they did not receive the undivided attention and parental guidance children needed growing up. Monica and Morris were way too absorbed in their social lives to provide the girls with the focus that children required. Tom and she were unable to have children of their own, so now was her chance to nurture and possibly make a lasting, positive impression on Maggie's and Macie's lives.

At first, Mary thought they might be thinking of settling down in North Falls, but since their unannounced visit, they seemed increasingly moody and restless. More than anything she wanted them to stay to witness firsthand her importance in the community and, hopefully, carry that message back to their mother.

She wanted to offer the girls a bit of holiday cheer to make them feel more at home and decided some festive touches in their private rooms would be just the trick to bridge the growing distance between them. They hadn't been easy to get along with lately, and she suspected their restlessness ran deeper than just missing their familiar surroundings. Still it struck her as odd, and a little peculiar, that they showed up without so much as a letter or phone call to say they were coming for the holidays.

It hadn't been Mary's intention to go snooping in their rooms this morning. Her goal was to surprise her nieces. She had purchased several beautiful figurines, fluffy holiday pillows for the beds and lounging chairs, along with garland and soft white lights to string along the dressers, doorways, and headboards. Mary was a gifted decorator, and her home was, without exception, always magazine-ready.

As the girls left for work that morning, Mary had eagerly entered Macie's room first. It was immaculate, which pleased her aunt. After completing the finishing touches, she took a step back and admired her handiwork. Who wouldn't be thrilled to have a room as glamorous as this? she thought.

She quickly moved to Maggie's bedroom, carrying the remaining garnishments. As she entered, she noticed the girls kept different housekeeping habits. While the room wasn't exactly cluttered, it lacked the pristine tidiness of Macie's. Her eyes were immediately drawn to the closet door, which stood slightly ajar. On closer inspection, she discovered a tiny scuff mark on the doorframe. It was a minor detail, but enough to spark a flicker of alarm. She knew without a doubt everything had been in immaculate condition. These rooms were rarely used. She opened the closet and immediately noticed the myriad of shoe boxes lying helter-skelter across the closet floor. Her instincts were on alert; something felt off. She had a tiny inkling that Maggie was hiding something. Kneeling down, she cautiously rearranged the jumbled mess, careful not to disturb Maggie's belongings. And that's when she saw it.

***

As Elizabeth and Grace walked through the snowy street, soft flecks of snow cascaded around them. Elizabeth finally lowered her phone. Her shoulders slumped, weighed down by a disarming disappointment she could no longer disguise.

"Elizabeth, whatever is wrong?" asked Grace, gently brushing a stray hair from Elizabeth's face.

"That was Eva and Ava. They won't be coming home for Christmas." Elizabeth tried to mask her letdown, but after everything that was happening, this jarring news felt as if it were too much to bear. Suddenly, she felt utterly drained.

"So they won't be home for Christmas," said Grace despondently.

"Something came up at work," said a dishearten Elizabeth.

"Oh, Elizabeth, it's okay if you're disappointed that they won't be coming home. It's a natural reaction after all the planning you've done to make it a perfect holiday getaway, so don't feel bad about the way you feel. Just don't let your sorrow drown your spirit for the holidays."

Elizabeth's features were laden in despair, and her posture sagged in resignation.

"Listen, you know the Morgan sisters always have each other," said Grace reassuringly. "We'll have a sparkling holiday with all the trimmings. I know it won't be the same without the twins, but this is the new reality. We've got to let them live their own lives."

Grace was heartbroken too, but she did her best to camouflage her disappointment that was growing steadily in the pit of her stomach. She knew how much Elizabeth had been counting on her daughters returning home to share in the holiday joy and wished there were a magic wand she could wave to ease her sister's discouragement. She reached over to give her sibling a hug and then took her hand as they moseyed toward the Sugar Bowl. It was such an endearing sight, two aging comrades, leaning on each other and silently commiserating in their shared gloom, as a cloud of dismay hovered above them, stubborn and crushing. But, no doubt, Beryl would know exactly what to do to uplift the spirits of her beloved siblings.

As the two members of the Morgan Sisters Sleuthing Club sauntered down the street, preoccupied by their own thoughts, they were oblivious to the individual who was watching them intently, and that person was determined to discover just how much they knew.

Perched in the shadow of a recessed doorway, the figure remained perfectly still, blending effortlessly into the background like a forgotten detail. His eyes were sharp, calculating. Every gesture, every glance exchanged between Elizabeth and Grace were noted, absorbed, and filed away with a ruthless efficiency.

Elizabeth gestured animatedly as she recounted their conversation with the mayor. It was important to keep her mind busy to help distract her from the ache left by the twins' news. Her voice, carried by the wind, was easily heard. "Grace, there is something he's not telling us. Something's off... *way off.*"

The figure stiffened. There it was. The sisters suspected something. Maybe not everything, but enough to make them a threat.

15

Close Encounters of the Worst Kind

After an enchanting chat with her beloved family, Elizabeth pushed back from the table after inhaling bread pudding topped with heavy cream and hot coffee that tasted like heaven. Beryl knew not only what to say to lift her sisters' spirits but also how to keep their tummies joyous as well.

"Are you feeling better, dear?" asked Beryl hopefully, as she wiped a crumb from the table.

"Oh, goodness, yes. In fact, I'm quite excited about their new endeavor. I just needed some time to put it all into perspective. Can you just imagine what they must be feeling? I'm sure they're over the moon!" gushed Elizabeth.

From the moment they were born, two tiny, wriggling bundles wrapped in identical pink blankets, Elizabeth had felt an instant, soul-deep connection. She had watched them grow, not just into beautiful young women, but into each other's mirror, complementing where the other fell short, finishing each other's sentences, speaking in a language only they truly understood. But she had always been part of that language. Always included, always needed. Until now.

She could still hear their laughter echoing down the upstairs hallway, see them sprawled across the living room rug, Ava singing, Eva plucking at her guitar, both of them tossing popcorn into each other's mouths, and dragging her into whatever nonsense they were dreaming up. They were her joy. Her heartbeat. Her home.

Surrounding her were the soft clinks of silverware and the quiet murmur of voices that reminded her she wasn't entirely alone. But there were times when Elizabeth felt like a single note ringing out in the distance with no one there to hear.

"Well," began Grace, breaking Elizabeth's reverie, "we should be expecting our little detective agency any minute. I can't wait to see Finch's face when you tell him what we discovered."

"Me either. It will be a sweet moment!" exclaimed Elizabeth, who couldn't help but break into a devious smile.

Just at that moment, the novice investigators trailed in, one by one. As the hungry group sat down, Grace was practically thumping with anticipation to get the show on the road. "Is everyone ready for Elizabeth's new development?"

"I knew something was up. Let's hear it! I've been as jumpy as a cat on a hot tin roof!" said Peg in that wonderful comic way of hers that no one else could ever master.

As Beryl placed the bread pudding and steaming coffee before each individual, Elizabeth began.

"We discovered that Mary Beeman does, in fact, own the mysterious sports car."

"The red one with the tinted windows?" Beryl asked, her voice edged with suspicion. She sensed the forthcoming information was going to expose a somber truth.

"That's the one," affirmed Grace, trying, but failing, to suppress the crackle in her voice. She was imploding with the thrill of what they had uncovered. It felt good to be ahead of the curve for once. Finch and Ana weren't the only ones doing their homework.

Beryl leaned back in her chair, the old wood creaking beneath her, and folded her arms, awaiting what was yet to be revealed.

"Well, the mayor affirmed that the meeting at the bank was indeed concerning the go-ahead with the complex, despite the voters' opinion. Curtis is dead set on getting that project started and completed."

"That crackbrain just won't give up. That's underhanded and dishonest," complained Peg, as she smacked her lips from the tasty dessert and uttered a sigh of contentment.

"It's nothing we didn't already expect," reminded Beryl.

"What's this car got to do with anything?" Finch asked, quite perplexed.

"That's the car Elizabeth saw drive off with Curtis on its tail, following the after-hours meeting with the mayor at the bank," reminded Grace, her voice full of animation.

"Oh, yes...thank you for reminding me," Finch replied politely, as his face took on a look that said his brain was furiously trying to follow the thread.

"This car, according to the mayor, is an Alfa Romeo 33 Stradale. Isn't that what Tom said, Grace?"

"Yes. Go on," said Grace, urging her on. She couldn't wait to see Finch's and the others' reactions.

"This same car was parked in back of Powell's office earlier today. Mary Beeman was there to see...are you ready?" Gosh, thought Elizabeth, realizing she just pulled a Finch stunt and gave a slight shudder.

"Yes, please continue," said Finch as patiently as he could. He would rather curl up and die than let Elizabeth know he was on the edge of his seat.

Oh, now you want to get on with the story, thought Elizabeth. Humph, I can play this game too...only better. The nerve of that man!

"The receptionist is..." There was a dramatic pause. "none other than Mary Beeman's niece, Maggie Dolman!" Elizabeth's voice rose just a little for added effect. "*And* she has a sister named Macie who works as a maid at the Holly Hill, *and...* Macie was working the night of the murder!" Take that Finch!

"And that's not all!" chimed in Grace. "Keep going, Elizabeth."

"My, there's more?" stated Finch, not being able to believe his ears.

"Oh, yes," said Grace, "and guess where they grew up? Tell 'em, Elizabeth."

"I'm trying," replied Elizabeth, hoping she wouldn't lose her momentum by Grace's overeager interruptions. "Maggie and Macie are Morris and Monica Dolman's daughters. They grew up in...London and were educated at Oxford. May I remind you that..."

"Bartholomew was British!" Grace cut in, bursting with yet another enthusiastic interruption.

Finch just sat there, spoon to his pale face, mouth agape, as Peg, Beryl, and Ana tried to process the plethora of information.

Oh, thought Elizabeth. His expression is priceless! Finch one, Elizabeth a thousand. This is a slam dunk!

"These sisters..." nodded Beryl slowly, eyes narrowing and her crow's feet becoming more pronounced. "Things are starting to fit, aren't they?"

"I need to do something. Please excuse me," mumbled Ana, already on her feet. "I'll be back shortly," and, with that, she quickly exited the diner.

"She must be going to check on something. This is getting good!" declared Peg, practically bouncing in her seat.

"I'm just shell-shocked that you two gathered so much information in such a very short amount of time," gasped Beryl. "Well, I'm just flabbergasted!"

"Finch, what do you have to say?" asked Grace innocently.

"I'm totally..."

"Gobsmacked?" interrupted Elizabeth.

"No, I was going to say..."

"Jealous?"

"Impressed. You two certainly need to be congratulated," Finch said fondly.

"Well, now I'm dumbfounded," responded Elizabeth, as a slow grin began to grow. "Yes, we brought home the bacon today."

While the friends were asking questions, all at the same time, mulling over the information, and what it could mean; across town, Mary Beeman was making one final stop.

***

Mary Beeman was not home when Elizabeth and Grace knocked on her door earlier. She was racing to the inn to talk with Macie after getting nowhere with Maggie at the realtor's office. Mary was in a panic and needed a viable explanation for what she had discovered.

The North Falls' first lady, pulled into the Holly Hill Inn's parking lot as close to the front door as she could. She was in a dead panic to find Macie as quickly as possible. She was sure Maggie had already called ahead to fill Macie in on their altercation at the realtor's office and was terrified that Macie would make a run for it. Mary was sure the girls were up to no good, but she refused to believe they had anything to do with something illegal. There had to be a plausible explanation for what she found in the closet. There simply had to be! Oh, the scandal! The shame! Mary's mind was working overtime on how to rectify a potential crisis and quickly, before her husband found out.

***

Mary was correct in her assumption, for Maggie wasted no time in relaying the chaos to her sister that occurred at the realtor's office by their burner phones. Between their aunt's discovery and the unexpected visit of Mrs. Davis, it was Maggie who was ready to bolt.

***

Mayor Beeman was near hysteria himself. The Morgan sisters were much farther along in their novice investigation than he could ever have imagined. How in the world did they figure out so much so quickly? He felt as if his whole world were crashing down around him, and none of this was his fault. Oh, how would he ever explain this to his wife?

***

Macie was quite careful as she left the inn just as her boring nitwit aunt entered the establishment. It was quite easy to evade her, for Macie knew all the ins and outs of the old hotel, of which she had been exploring since her arrival. She also had Maggie secretly make two sets of spare keys to the coveted car, one for each of them just in case they ever needed a quick getaway. A fox always has an escape route if it wants to outsmart its prey. As she exited from a side entrance, she stealthily maneuvered herself like a greased silk ribbon to the side of Mary's prized vehicle, inserted her spare key, and off she flew into the wild blue yonder.

***

Mary called her husband's office as a last-ditch effort and interrupted a very important meeting with none other than Curtis Hughes and a group of his cronies, all vying for the much needed approval of the mayor for the newly introduced project expansion. Tom had left specific instructions with his secretary, Greta James, that he was not to be disturbed under any circumstances. Curtis was beyond desperate to get this complex approved and moving forward that he had pulled in the big guns with the big money. After speaking with her boss' frenzied wife, Greta took it upon herself to barge into the private gathering and announce to the entire group that Tom had to leave immediately due to an unexpected family emergency. As he followed Mrs. James from the conference room, she quickly explained her conversation with Mary and that he needed to hightail it out of there. For once, the mayor listened to his secretary.

***

Just as things were winding down at the Sugar Bowl, the diner's landline began to ring. Beryl left the table to prepare a to-go order while her comrades were exchanging goodbyes and finalizing plans for their next get-together. Everyone was tingling with anticipation and eager to unravel the puzzling events that had disrupted their holiday season.

"Grace, I'm going to take a walk," stated Elizabeth. "My head is spinning, and I need to think. I just know we're still missing something. It's niggling at the back of my mind, wrestling to get free."

"Mind if I go with you? Ivy's watching the store, and I need a good stroll too. Goodness, what a day! I'm frazzled," said Grace.

No one took much notice when Grace and Elizabeth grabbed their coats and left their chums still pondering the unexpected information and the excitement it had brought to their mundane lives.

As the sisters strolled down Main Street, they just missed Ana returning to the diner. Her face was pink from the cold, and red blotches had bloomed on her neck and chest, quiet possibly from the news she had just discovered.

"Guess what I found!" Ana sputtered with more emotion than anyone had ever seen.

"Well, don't just stand there," urged Peg. "Spill it!"

***

With no real destination in mind, the siblings, once again, found themselves wandering down Main Street, straight toward Powell Realty. "Elizabeth, look in the back parking lot! See that?" asked Grace, barely able to contain herself. And sure enough, there again was the red Alfa Romeo 33 Stradale, parked haphazardly behind the building.

"I'm going in to see exactly who is driving that car," said Elizabeth, like a determined warrior raging into battle, and off she went like a jackrabbit with Grace racing to keep up.

This time they slipped undetected through the back door that Mayor Beeman used on Grace's prior visit. As the slippery sleuths quietly crept down the ill-lit hallway, they heard bits and pieces of a muted conversation. As they wormed their way as close as they dared, an altercation was clearly in progress. Maggie and Macie were about to have an all-out brawl.

"Maggie, stop it!" Macie snapped. "You don't know anything for sure. You're freaking out over nothing. Just stay calm."

"I'm telling you everything's unraveling," Maggie cried. "It's happening all over again."

"No, it's not," Macie said firmly. "We stick to the plan, and we'll be fine."

***

As Mayor Beeman pulled up to the Holly Hill Inn, he spotted his wife standing near the front entrance with Virginia Pierce, who appeared to be unsuccessfully comforting her. Mary was visibly shaken, wringing her hands in a desperate attempt to control her nerves, but to Tom, it was obvious she was deeply agitated. The mayor abruptly got out of his ancient American-made vehicle and hurried to his wife's side.

"Virginia! Holly Hill looks incredible," he said, his voice overly cheerful. "I was just telling Mary this morning how the whole town's been raving about what you and Ed have done with the inn," he cooed, trying to mask his distress and frustration at being pulled from his private meeting with the influential businessmen.

Turning toward Mary, he asked, "Is everything alright, dear?"

"Oh, yes, darling," she replied with a weak smile. "I just starting to feel a bit lightheaded and thought it best to have you drive me home. I didn't think it was wise for me to get behind the wheel. Virginia was sweet enough to stay with me even though I told her not to trouble herself. I'm feeling better now." The lie clung to her like cheap perfume.

"Oh, it was no trouble at all. What are friends for? Are you sure you're alright? I could bring you a glass of water or maybe some juice?" offered Virginia, sycophantically.

"No, no, I'm fine, really," Mary insisted. "You go and take care of your guests. We'll be in for dinner soon."

"We should schedule a pickleball match at the club!" Virginia chirped, all but forgetting Mary's misery. "I hear it's all the rage!" she said beaming, clearly thrilled to be rubbing shoulders with the North Falls' elite.

"Come on, Mary," Tom said tenderly, steering her toward the car. "Thanks for looking after her, Virginia."

"Oh, it was no trouble. I'll call you soon," Virginia trilled after them, as Tom loaded Mary up in the passenger seat and climbed in beside her. Once they pulled away, Tom's tone shifted.

"Mary, what on earth happened, and where's your car?" Clutching the fabric of her skirt, she took a ragged breath, and began the terrifying tale.

***

Ana entered the Sugar Bowl out of breath and full of information, looking like a determined angel who had just landed to bring gifts to the multitudes.

"Ana, you remind me of the cat that killed the canary," said Beryl, eyeing her with amused suspicion.

"I don't think it was a canary that those kittens killed," remarked Ana coolly, a flicker of something unreadable in her eyes.

"What do you mean by that?" asked Peg, clearly puzzled by the pun.

"You found something," Finch stated, his voice steady with confidence.

Ana nodded her head as everyone gathered around the table, bracing themselves for the bombshell she was about to drop.

Ana sat down and spread several printed pages across the table.

"Well, for goodness' sake, what did you find?" asked Peg. "I'm too old for such suspense."

"I downloaded this from the library's digital archives, made copies for everyone, and then cleared the browser and the printer history, so there's no trace. Don't worry, Mrs. Evans..." Ana looked around, noticing Elizabeth's absence. "Wait, where is Mrs. Evans?"

"I saw her and Grace sneak out for a walk. They probably didn't want to get another lecture from big sis," chuckled Peg.

"If they get into any more trouble," warned Beryl, "I'm going to lock them up! Those two worry me to death."

Ana quickly passed each a copy of her findings, as the novice crime solvers began perusing the documents. She then gave a brief synopsis of the case file. "According to the British press, two unidentified women were being pursued for questioning by Scotland Yard in connection to a jewelry heist in west London. Although the women have not yet been charged with any illegal activity, they allegedly fled the country, baffling the Metropolitan Police."

"Wait, I have a ..." began Peg

"Hold on, let's let her finish." Finch had a strong inkling that the best was yet to come. He leaned forward, his instincts tingling. He knew Ana much better than the rest of the group, for they had been working closely together since the investigation began. He knew she would hold the most significant piece of information till the very end, and he was right. His once shy, backward sidekick was picking up confidence with each successful assignment.

Ana took a deep breath and placed another document on the table. "I found this next bit of information while digging through...Scotland Yard's internal files," Ana paused, bracing herself for a lecture, but no one batted an eye. Ana's questionable hacking habits were not only expected, they were trusted by the sleuthing club, for she had proved she really was very *very* good at what she did.

"Richard Gerald Bartholomew, also known as Marshall Wymark, our murder victim, was a former chief inspector. Highly decorated. In his later years, he worked undercover on highly classified assignments. I won't go into all of them, but one in particular stands out." She paused, looking around the table.

He was assigned to the west London jewelry heist. The victims of that robbery were socialites who moved in the same social circles as Mr. and Mrs. Morris Dolman." She glanced around the table, letting the information sink in. "This was Mr. Bartholomew's final assignment. He was planning to retire once the case was closed. According to the files, he was hot on their trail. An arrest was believed to be imminent. I believe Maggie and Macie are our mystery women from the west London heist," replied Ana solemnly.

"Oh, dear," said Beryl, expecting trouble.

"So that's the connection. At last," breathed Finch.

***

Elizabeth and Grace stood frozen as the Dolman sisters continued their heated conversation.

"Look," Macie said slowly, as if explaining to a child, "Powell had to go, just like Bartholomew. We didn't have a choice, and you know it."

There was a sharp intake of breath as Grace realized what the girls had just revealed. Elizabeth quickly pressed her finger to her lips to remind Grace to watch her reactions.

"You should've consulted me before putting the jewels in the office safe!" chastised Macie.

"I told you it's never used!" Maggie shot back defensively. "It was a brilliant idea. If someone found them, Powell would take the fall, and Curtis would still collect the insurance money, while we'd disappear with his jewels. There wouldn't be a thing he could do about it. There was nothing wrong with that plan."

In the hallway, Grace and Elizabeth exchanged a wary look. They knew staying hidden was dangerous, but, with an understanding nod, they agreed to take the risk and remain where they were in order to get to the truth.

"And yet," Macie hissed, "somehow James figured out the stash was in his office safe. So big brave Curtis had you move it to your *bedroom closet???* where Aunt Mary could stumble upon it! Are you kidding me? How *dumb* could you be?"

"Well, if you had a better idea, you should have said so. How did James even find out? That's not on me," Maggie retorted.

"I have no idea," Macie growled, "but Powell somehow suspected you were having an affair with that senile banker and confronted Curtis at the gala. I just happened to be standing right next to them and heard every word. Then *I* had to clean up their champaign mess." Macie was getting angrier by the minute, recalling the most humiliating incident of her life. Her face began to reddened as she remembered Virginia Pierce snapping her fingers at her and then pointing to the muck on the floor. She had felt like a dog in obedience class.

"Listen! We were *very* discreet. You didn't seem to complain when I handed over his mother's fancy heirlooms. He was just *so* easy to play. So trusting. Poor little idiot. Tsk-tsk," responded Maggie maliciously, hoping to transfer Macie's wrath onto Curtis.

"And you're *sure* this place isn't bugged?" Macie asked suddenly.

"Yes! I swept the entire office with a fine-tooth comb the day I got hired. No cameras. Who in their right mind would bother installing surveillance in a loser realty office anyway?"

"Well, his *house* had a state-of-the-art system."

"Well, you and the snowstorm took care of that, remember? So relax."

"I never relax," Macie replied cooly. "That's why we've never been caught."

"Yes, you're just *so* competent," replied Maggie with a sarcastic sneer that tainted her beauty. "That's why James had to be disposed of, right?"

"He was a necessary casualty that *you* could have prevented."

"Oh, don't you dare put that on me!" Maggie shot back.

"Well, it doesn't matter now," Macie said coldly. "It's time to deal with dear old auntie pain-in-the-bum, act heartbroken, cry like fools at her funeral, and then get the heck out of this tiny little town."

"What do you mean? Aunt Mary won't say anything. That'd ruin her perfect reputation," scoffed Maggie.

"Come on, Maggie. You aren't *that* naive, are you?" Macie's voice turned to ice. "I've been planning what we'd do if it ever came to this, and, thanks to *you*, now it has." Maggie flinched at her sister's accusatory tone.

"What about the jewels? We can't just leave them at Aunt Mary's."

"After your call, I went back and moved them. They're in the trunk of her car. Tonight, once it's dark, we'll put them back in the safe. In the meantime, I've got a sob story ready for dear auntie to buy us some time. I know exactly how we'll play this. And once everything's in place, we'll need another Santa suit. Now lock up."

"Wow," Maggie muttered, with a hint of respect. "You really do have a Plan B."

Elizabeth and Grace were quaking with fear as they heard this last bit of testimony. Elizabeth quietly gestured for them to back out before they were caught red-handed. But wouldn't you know it? The floor creaked, and the office screamed with silence.

***

After Mary Beeman finished her ghastly story, the mayor was fraught with panic. There was nothing else to do. He lifted his phone and made the most devastating call of his political life. "Listen, they've also stolen my wife's car and could be anywhere. You have to find them. I'm trusting you to take care of this," the mayor emphasized emphatically. And with that, he hung up.

***

"Well, if it isn't Batman and Robin. You and your meddlesome nursing-home assistants have been nothing but a nuisance since the Christmas gala," snarled Macie, her words dripping like acid.

Elizabeth lunged for the door just as it flew open from the other side, slamming violently into her. Maggie stood in the doorway, eyes seething with fury. Without a word, she shoved them so forcefully that Grace stumbled, crashing hard against the wall. The hallway suddenly seemed to close in around them, no exit, no way out. Panic clawed its way in, making breathing difficult.

"I should have killed your little mutt when I had the chance. Maybe then you would have stopped playing detective," Maggie said vindictively. "If it were up to me, that's exactly what would have happened."

"*You* broke into my house?" Elizabeth couldn't believe what her brain was telling her. "Why would you harm my dog?"

"To stop your snooping," flared Maggie. "And I would've too, but my sister can't stand to see an animal hurt. Lucky you." She gave a mocking smile. "You should probably thank her...while you still can."

Elizabeth turned sharply to face Macie. "You'd kill a person, but draw the line at a dog?"

"Elizabeth," cautioned Grace. This was a Maggie she had not seen before, and, frankly, it terrified her.

"Wait a minute," said Elizabeth, her brain reeling. "My neighbor said it was a man. Was someone else with you?"

"Nope." Maggie grinned malevolently. "Just me. I'm a master of disguise," she bragged. "It's amazing what a man's coat and a little twilight can do."

Macie stepped forward, lips curling. "Well, looks like we'll need more Santa suits."

Elizabeth's heart dropped.

"I have a spare one stashed away at Hughes's house. I'll drop Officer Ruff a hint. I'm sure he'll find it," Macie added smoothly.

"Curtis's?" Maggie blinked, then her expression shifted from puzzlement to admiration. "Oh, I get it."

"Yep, that suit links your darling lover to the murder of Santa Claus. Case closed," and Macie winked, oh, so wickedly. Elizabeth clenched her fist. She wanted nothing more than to slap that arrogant smirk right off Macie's face.

***

Tom Beeman had called the only person who could take care of such matters. Otherwise, who knows what would have happened to his devious nieces and their innocent victims? This individual immediately spied the 33 Stradale in its askew parking space. He was watching the entire escapade unfold from his phone, thanks to a live security feed, as he stood in the alley of the Woolly Lamb. James Powell had informed him of his state-of-the-art security system at his home, as well as the one secretly hidden in his office, as soon as he suspected something was off with Maggie and Curtis. Thankfully he took the required precautions in a timely fashion.

Upon hearing James's suspicion of his new receptionist, Officer Ruff downloaded the feed from the security system onto his smartphone to keep an eye on Maggie Dolman and her suspected lover, Curtis Hughes. He was also the individual who was closely watching Elizabeth and Grace as they left Mayor Beeman's office earlier. Yes, Officer Ruff was a shrewd man of the law, but fortunately for Elizabeth and Grace, he was about to become their Superman.

Cora and Janice, co-owners of the Keep Me in Stitches shop, were correct in their assessment of Officer Ruff. He was the sharpest knife in a drawer of many weapons.

Officer Ruff crept quietly to the outlandish sports car and professionally popped open the driver's door. Reaching in, he diligently disarmed it by pulling the fuse to the ignition system, and just to make doubly sure the car wouldn't start, he also removed the battery cable. Not bad for a Barney Fife.

As the infamous sisters and their terrified hostages skirted around the office building in the early evening shadows, Officer Ruff was patiently biding his time leaning on the passenger's side door. He looked just like an easygoing Sheriff Andy Taylor on a lazy Sunday afternoon.

"Well, evening, ladies." Gracious goodness! He even sounded like the Mayberry sheriff with his slow Southern drawl! "Planning a joy ride, are we? If you are, you might want to loosen that grip you got on our fine residents, and let me drive my car." Holding up his phone for all to see the live feed on his cam app, he smiled and gestured, "Right this way, ladies."

Maggie and Macie exchanged a glance, calculation flashing in their eyes, but Office Ruff didn't even flinch. He just smiled and said, "Don't even think about it."

By using the element of surprise, Officer Ruff apprehended and handcuffed the Dolman sisters without so much as a gunshot. In fact, it was as easy as taking candy from a baby. So much for the international jewel thieves and Scotland Yard to boot.

***

It was sometime later when Elizabeth and Grace were finally released to go home. Between interrogating sessions of the notorious sisters, Officer Ruff kindly kept the Morgan gals abreast as new information was revealed.

After an tiring stretch of questions and explanations, Elizabeth and Grace slowly made their way from the interview rooms and past the security gate, where their entourage was waiting on hard-backed chairs and looking as exhausted as the sisters felt.

"Oh, girls. Are you alright? Beryl's waiting for me to call so she can get your supper ready, and we're dying to know all the details," Peg said, wringing her hands and thumping her feet.

"Only if you're up for it, of course. You've had quite the experience," reasoned Finch.

"Well," began Grace, "as tired as I am, I couldn't possibly go to bed until the story is told. Let's go."

"Yes, let's get out of here," agreed Peg. "My back is killing me."

"And I'm starving," chimed in Elizabeth. And off they went, arm in arm to the best little diner in all the village.

16

Case Closed

The diner was closed to privately accommodate the sleuthing club and celebrate the apprehension of the scoundrels that had plagued their village. Beryl had prepared roast beef open-faces, warm apple sauce, and banana pudding to calm the trauma of today's activities.

"Well, I hope this doesn't deter the tourists from coming to visit Snowflake Village. Isn't it such a shame?" lamented Peg. "Two murders and a jewelry heist! I just can't wrap my head around it."

"I was worried sick. You two need a good spanking for traipsing off like that without a word. What in the world were you thinking?" scolded Beryl, the mother hen of her siblings and the biggest doom seeker of them all.

"Before Beryl gets out her hickory switch, I have a few questions I'd like answered, if you're up to it," Finch asked pensively.

"We'll start with the sequence of events that we know, and then we'll answer any questions you may have. Officer Ruff promised to fill us in sometime tomorrow morning on what he discovers from the interrogations, and then we'll meet back here to discuss what we've learned," announced Elizabeth, looking very businesslike, and resembling the disciplinarian she once was.

No, this wasn't quite police protocol, but it was North Falls, and Officer Ruff felt obligated to give the sisters first dibs on the developments since the case would soon be officially closed. Later that evening the riffraff would be booked and processed. He was expecting the press to be knocking on his door any moment. This was a huge story, and the *North Falls Standard* wouldn't be the only paper hounding him for details. The whole village was already abuzz, but he felt the sisters, due to their intense involvement, had a right to hear it straight from him before it hit the news circuit.

Before Elizabeth and Grace took turns explaining the sequence of events they overheard from the hallway, Beryl informed the friends that Ana had other obligations and would drop in later to help with the cleaning up. Beryl promised she would fill her in on all the developments. With that, the curious sleuths were ready to hear the gruesome details.

"So much has happened, I'm not even sure where to start," said Grace, pumped from the blasted ordeal.

"Let's start as to how James Powell came to hire Maggie as his receptionist," recommend Beryl.

"Well, apparently, quite by accident," said Grace, picking up the thread. "Tom Beeman was actually looking for another home, but not to downsize, to expand for a more regal home fit for the mayor of North Falls. He was interested in the old Cadwallader mansion, after next year's election, of course. James happened to mention that Cheryl Therry was about to retire, so Tom took the opportunity to call in a favor and asked if he would hire Maggie, his favorite of his wife's nieces, who was new to town and looking for employment."

"That's tough to swallow. James did a favor for Tom and look where it got him! Poor kid," said Peg, shaking her head.

"And poor timing," added Finch, quietly.

As Elizabeth and Grace continued, they revealed that Officer Ruff reported James had discovered furtive meetings taking place between Curtis and Maggie from the minuscule and very well disguised security cameras hidden in, of all places, the wainscoting. When James continued to view the surreptitious after-hours get-togethers from his phone app, his suspicions were confirmed. They were having a romantic relationship. But that wasn't all.

"James witnessed Curtis bringing the "alleged" stolen items to his office for Maggie to store in what she believed was an unused office safe. It was actually used to store ancient legal documents before everything was digitized, so she was right. It wasn't used and really should have been removed ages ago. James sneaked back to the office after closing to confirm that the bag did indeed hold the stolen jewels. He correctly put two and two together and surmised they were planning to put the blame solely on him if their plan backfired," finished Elizabeth, who was revved up and itching to tell all they had learned earlier from the policeman.

"And, of course, that was the plan," confirmed Beryl, who shook her head at the malicious intent.

"So this must have been when James alerted Officer Ruff," said Finch, who was mesmerized by the telling of how the clues were, at last, all fitting together.

"Correct," related Grace. "Curtis was keeping his distance from James for obvious reasons, so James confronted him at the gala hoping a crowd would keep the conversation civil. Unfortunately, Hughes told Powell it was none of his business.

This caused James to lose his temper and tell Hughes that if he were going to use his secretary to store stolen property in his office safe, then it was most certainly his business. That's when the altercation grew more vehement, and Curtis accidentally knocked into the waiter who spilled the champaign."

"Oh, the dreaded party scene. I had a feeling there was more to it," said Peg, who was listening keenly to every word. Her hands were shaking as she continued shredding a napkin to a fare-thee-well as the tiny pieces were making quite the mess on the tabletop.

"James then relayed Curtis and Maggie's relationship to his ole buddy, Mayor Beeman. Although James and Tom were both appalled at the inappropriate age difference, the mayor was livid. I'm positive that was the topic being discussed when I interrupted them on my last visit to the realty office. I knew something was up," surmised Grace.

"So, I'm guessing that was the gist of the after-hours meeting at the bank that Elizabeth witnessed between Curtis and Mayor Beeman," surmised Beryl.

"You're spot on, Beryl, as always" replied Elizabeth. "Tom told his wife what James had discovered, and Mary was mortified. She warned him not to tell a single soul for fear of a scandal and tarnishing their good name. That was why he lied to us and said the after-hours get-together was about pushing the project through. He was scared stiff Mary would tar and feather him if he ever let that leak out."

"So you can imagine how nervous he was when we showed up," added Grace.

"After James told Curtis he knew about his mother's stolen bling," continued Elizabeth, "Powell hoped Curtis would confess and come clean, which, as we all know, he didn't. Instead, Curtis panicked and told Maggie to move the jewels, which she hid in her bedroom closet.

"Unfortunately for the sisters, Mary Beeman happened upon the expensive trinkets when she planned to surprise her nieces with Christmas decorations in their bedrooms. That debacle hindered the plan for Maggie and Macie to make a clean getaway," finished Grace, who was looking slightly pale. Elizabeth and Grace privately decided to leave out the gory details. They believed talking about the planned murders reserved for Mary Beeman and themselves were too much to reveal after all the group had been through; plus, they secretly feared Beryl really would use the hickory switch.

"But why the Santa getups?" pondered Finch. He was impatient to get to the nitty gritty and give his mind a rest. He had spent every waking moment trying to figure out the uncanny specifics since Bartholomew's body was discovered at the gala.

"Hopefully, Officer Ruff can fill in the blanks tomorrow morning. I need to get home to my dog. He hasn't been let out since this morning." Elizabeth made her goodbyes as she left the table and made her way to get her coat.

"Elizabeth, you and Grace go on home. You need anything, call one of us. Finch, will you see the girls get home?"

"My pleasure, Beryl."

"I'm going too. So, we're to meet here tomorrow for our last powwow? I can't wait to know the nitty gritty at last," said Peg, as she slowly rose and unknowingly brushed a large smattering of napkin bits onto the floor.

"I'll call as soon as we're finished with Officer Ruff," promised Grace.

And with that, the four cronies made their way home through the gaily lit streets of North Falls.

***

Back at the police station, Officer Ruff was getting nowhere with the first suspect, Macie Dolman. Macie wouldn't even say, "No comment." She sat with her arms defiantly crossed around her chest and looked straight ahead, as though she were in a trance. No amount of pleading, cajoling, or any other tactical methods moved the stoic individual to assist in the interrogation.

Maggie was a whole other story. She grabbed the first deal that was offered and sang like a canary. Of course she blamed the entire scheme on her sister, which didn't fly with the savvy policeman. Officer Ruff was an ideal specialist when it came to unraveling a confession, and Maggie was more than a willing participate. When the terms of her crimes were communicated in a straightforward manner, Maggie had crumbled and disclosed the sisters' strategy step-by-step. After revealing the heinous acts, there was little hope of either sister seeing the light of day.

Curtis Hughes was appalled that he was handcuffed for all the residents of Sycamore Circle to witness. Once he became aware of the sisters' involvement with the deaths of Bartholomew and Powell, he felt pleading guilty to insurance fraud was a mild sentence compared to his unlawful partner, Maggie Dolman.

The three unsavory rogues were photographed, fingerprinted, and processed before midnight. Not a bad day's work for ole Barney Fife.

***

Finch insisted he escort Elizabeth and Grace to the police station first thing tomorrow morning. Grace found his desire to protect them endearing and was grateful for his genuine concern. It had been a long time since a man had gone out of his way to comfort her in times of distress. She didn't want to admit to anyone the terror she experienced in that darkened hallway, but it had taken a mighty toll on her nerves.

Elizabeth, on the other hand, felt Finch's unnecessary attention was a distraction. She could handle this prickly situation on her own without someone standing in the wings, holding her hand. She was a strong woman; however, if she were entirely honest, the genuine kindness and empathy Finch showed to her and and her sister stirred something within. Elizabeth liked being independent but wasn't ready to leave room for any kind of further involvement with the enigma Finch.

After seeing Grace to her door, Finch and Elizabeth made their way silently to her street. As her lane came into view, Elizabeth turned to her fellow investigator and carefully articulated her intent. "Finch, Grace and I appreciate your concern. We really do, but I hope you understand that this is something I have to face on my own. I'll call you when we're on our way to the diner. Okay? We'll fill everyone in once we're all together. I'll see you tomorrow. Good night, and thank you again." Elizabeth made strong eye contact with her companion, before turning away.

Finch wondered why she was so intent on keeping him at bay. He just wanted to offer his support and shield her from further peril, but obviously she was not ready to take their friendship any further. He was a patient and understanding man. He decided then and there he would back away to give her some time. He was not ready to surrender, at least not just yet.

"Elizabeth," he called, "if this is how you want to conclude this awful mess, then so be it." He then paused, and with a touch of humor in his voice, he uttered, "I think you just want to beat me to the punch." He gave her a weak smile and headed off on his own, alone.

***

Early the next morning, Elizabeth and Grace, wired with adrenaline and eager to have the nightmarish experience behind them, entered the police station. They didn't have to wait long before the desk sergeant escorted them down the narrow hallway to Officer Ruff's office. Grace was sure she saw a cockroach scurrying to a hidey-hole and shivered at the discomforting surroundings. Jimmy Ruff was busy behind a large metal army-green desk looking through paperwork that was scattered across the messy surface. Grace and Elizabeth were surprised by his appearance. They expected to see dark circles beneath droopy eyes, a shadow across his unshaven face, and crumpled clothing, but Officer Ruff looked as if he didn't have a care in the world. He was freshly shaven, and his uniform was so crisp and wrinkle-free, it would make any military official proud.

"Good morning, ladies. I appreciate your coming in so early. I hope you slept well. I have a lot to go over with you before the press conference, so let's get started."

After a benign admonition concerning the risks they took, Officer Ruff gave them the remaining fragments of a wretched, yet fascinating, story that if someone had predicted it, no one in North Falls would have believed a word of it. And yet, Elizabeth Evans and Grace Davis found themselves enmeshed in a tale too horrible for anyone in the tiny village to comprehend.

As they exited the station, filled with startling information, they made their calls on the way to the Sugar Bowl where their family and friends would soon be waiting to hear the conclusion of the stunning tale.

***

Warm cranberry-orange muffins sat in homespun baskets, adorned with colorful holiday towels, and rich hot coffee awaited the curious club members. The meeting was held once again in the back dining area, reserved for parties and private get-togethers. The anxiety, mixed with curiosity, permeated about the intimate space. When everyone was seated, Elizabeth began to brief them on what Officer Ruff had reported to her and Grace earlier, beginning with Macie's stubborn resolve to remain silent, and Maggie jumping at the opportunity to take a deal and revealing all to their celebrated Herculean hero, Officer Ruff.

"But why the Santa getups?" implored Finch, who simply couldn't contain himself any longer.

"Ah, yes, the abhorrent Santa charade," sighed Elizabeth. "This part is hard to talk about."

"Let me do it," said Grace, offering her younger sister a much needed emotional break. The specifics of this particular deed were unsettling for both women; still, Grace understood how deeply it weighed on Elizabeth, who had already endured so much emotional turmoil. "Macie, according to Maggie, mind you, thought it was 'insanely humorous' that whoever discovered Bartholomew's dead body all spruced up in the Christmas-themed costume would suffer psychological distress. Not to mention it would be a nice twist to throw off the police and leave a most interesting calling card," finished Grace.

"That girl has some serious issues," added Beryl with conviction.

"I'm with you on that one," Peg said, as she shook her head in disbelief and looked about for a spare napkin.

"Wait," said Finch, "what about your scarf? How did it get tangled up in all this mess?"

"Oh, yes, now we come to my infamous Christmas scarf. Macie, as you know, worked at the Holly Hill and had a master key to all the rooms. She was cleaning a room adjacent to the master suite that Ed and Virginia Pierce occupied. She overheard them arguing and opened their door just a smidgeon so she could hear their confrontation. Ed was furious. Pastor White had just met with him to divulge that Virginia had snatched yet another item, which, as we all know, was my holiday scarf. She had promised her husband, before they relocated to North Falls, that she would never do such a thing again, especially after they had purchased the grand hotel and was easing into an elite social life here. It was supposed to be a new start for them both.

"Virginia is apparently very hard to work for and rode Macie every day about her lackadaisical attitude. So when Macie discovered Virginia's secret vice, she jumped at the chance to serve her a slice of humble pie. Macie witnessed the scarf in Pastor White's hand as he arrived quite early to the gala and correctly assumed it was the scarf in question that caused Ed to go apoplectic. She kept the reverend in her sight until she saw where he hid the scarf. Everyone was in such a tizzy getting the inn ready for the party, Macie just waltzed in, swiped it from Virginia's office drawer, and no one was the wiser. She wrapped the stolen scarf around poor Bartholomew's neck to incriminate and embarrass her uppity, spiteful boss in front of the whole town. Unfortunately, that vindictive act is what brought me into the murder mess," finished Elizabeth.

"I bet she wished she never saw that scarf," huffed Grace.

"That was pretty diabolical!" said Peg, cocking her head, as she glanced around, desperate for something to shred.

"What's going to happen to the Beemans and Curtis?" Beryl asked.

"Well, it seems as though Tom won't be running for another term as mayor, and Mary is so humiliated she's begging him to relocate...somewhere far away," Grace informed them.

"Curtis pleaded guilty and was arrested for insurance fraud. He was planning to invest the money in that dag gum mall. Not surprising, is it? That was one reason he pushed the project so hard. The other is poor old Curtis, president of the North Falls Community Bank, who is so community-oriented," Elizabeth said, lifting an eyebrow with mild sarcasm, "is basically broke. This mall was supposed to be his saving grace. The ten thousand dollars he offered to Ollie was a down payment from his investors to seal the deal. That was why he was so upset when Ollie refused to side with them on the expansion."

"Yahoo! Good for Ollie!" echoed Peg.

"Powell did not contribute to the bribe money, but he knew exactly where it came from and kept his mouth shut. He needed this project to go forward for financial gain as well and to move himself up the social ladder *without* any assistance from his very wealthy wife."

"And as for the Dolman girls, you can pretty well guess where they'll be spending their time," added Grace.

"Well, that pretty much sums it up. We were so lucky that James contacted Officer Ruff, and he followed his instinct. I'll never doubt him. He's a proven bloodhound," said Elizabeth, with a note of optimism in her demeanor.

"Did you find out why they vandalized Grace's furniture and tried to break in your house? I still get chills thinking about your poor little traumatized pup." Peg, too, loved dogs and had a special affinity for the collie breed. She kept her blue collie Tara indoors and couldn't imagine what she would do if someone would intentionally harm her.

"In hopes those acts would scare us so badly we would stop snooping. Obviously, they don't know the Morgan sisters," smiled Grace with a snap to her voice.

"When they brought my dog into it, they stepped over the line. I wasn't going to rest until I knew who was behind that," swore Elizabeth.

"You know, I have to admit I was surprised it was Maggie who wanted to harm Abner. My money would have been on Macie," said Grace, who had taken kindly to the young secretary.

"Thank goodness there was a soft place in Macie's heart for animals. I shudder to think what I would have done if...Anything else, guys?" asked Elizabeth, hoping to circumvent the discussion away from her pet.

"I have one last question. What was the secret that Hughes and Powell were holding over Ollie's head to get him to back the project?" Finch asked, inquisitively.

"I have no idea. That never came up," concluded Elizabeth.

"That is an odd piece of the puzzle, yet unsolved," pondered Finch. "We may never know."

If they're counting on me to blow the gaff, thought Grace, it's never going to happen.

***

After everyone said their goodbyes and Beryl got one last scolding in, the exhausted party headed their separate ways. Grace peeled off first, and then it was Elizabeth's turn.

"What an unbelievable morning!" she declared, as she and Finch made their way to her familiar street.

"What an adventure, you mean. I thought those days were behind me. I guess one never knows where life will take you," philosophized Finch.

"What an adventure is right," smiled Elizabeth. "I guess you'll be coming to Beryl's for Christmas dinner? She told me she invited you to partake in a good old Welsh Christmas."

"Noon on the dot. Are you okay with her inviting me?" Finch was hoping for something that would give him a spark of hope.

"Well, she's the Christmas boss. If she invited you, I guess it's all right by me. Until our next adventure."

"So you're hoping to see more of me then?" He was pushing it, and he knew it.

"Only if adventure calls." And with that, Elizabeth climbed the steps, unlocked the door, and silently thought, I hope it does.

17

Conclusion

Christmas Bells Are Ringing

Later that evening, Elizabeth tried to read a Christmas mystery over a light supper, but her mind was still reeling. After completing her nightly routine, she went to bed a little later than usual, her beloved Abner snuggled beneath the covers beside her. She was just drifting off, the promise of sweet dreams hovering, when an unexpected noise startled her awake. She sat up, trembling. Then a fire took root within her, a fierce spark of the bold, old Elizabeth resurfacing. This time, she would stand her ground. Clutching a candlestick, she stomped down the staircase toward the front door, refusing to cower before anyone who dared to invade her home at this ungodly hour. Abner was howling to a fare-thee-well just as the door creaked open...and then she heard the most glorious sound of all.

"Merry Christmas, Mom!"

Elizabeth gasped in surprise, one hand covering her mouth, while the other clutched at her heart. "Oh, my goodness! I can't believe it!" as Abner twirled around her feet.

Having her girls home was the best Christmas gift she could possibly imagine, and the only one that truly mattered. She hustled her offspring out of the cold, as Abner danced circles around their ankles, following his favorite humans indoors.

The twins stepped inside, wrapping their arms around their mother in a tight, perfect twin embrace. At a loss for words, Elizabeth finally found her voice. "I thought you were unable to come home for Christmas," she said, still catching her breath from the shock.

"The client and executive struggled to negotiate, bringing key elements of the project to a halt," Ava explained, barely pausing for breath, her words tumbling out in a flurry.

"And causing the project to get behind schedule," Eva continued with a note of irritation.

"I do believe stubborn and cantankerous egos were at play. Bah humbug," said Ava devilishly with a mischievous smile playing upon her lips.

"Yeah, we could've gotten home much earlier if the executive hadn't been such a Scrooge. Everyone knows the industry shuts down for winter break."

"Just as they finally settled on an agreement..." Ava began.

"an unexpected snowstorm was coming in," Eva interrupted, eyes sparkling with excitement.

"Not just a snowstorm. A blizzard!" said Ava emphatically. "Rescheduling the whole project due to the unforeseeable weather."

"Luckily, we flew out just in time," Eva murmured, relief threading through her voice.

"We're home!" the twins exclaimed in unison, jumping gleefully around their mother, as they did when they were small.

The earlier tension melted into the quiet movements of subdued nighttime routines: soft joyful laughter, feet padding across the wooden floors, and the soft clicking of Abner's nails trailing faithfully behind his beloved Elizabeth.

As the twins were, at last, settled in, a wave of gratitude washed over Elizabeth. Her girls were home! And for Elizabeth, this was the perfect icing on her Christmas cake.

***

As the snowplows cleared the narrow streets of Snowflake Village, the residents were out in full winter regalia the following morning, busy and excited doing last-minute shopping. As Ollie Williams made his way to the stitch shop, he was fairly sure Cora would have the lowdown. As he opened the door, he found her minding the store all alone.

"Where's Janice?" he asked.

"Oh, she had some last-minute errands to do before things get too crazy here," replied Cora. "How are you? I haven't seen you since all this crime excitement hit town." She smiled so sweetly at the elderly custodian he thought his heart would break.

"I stopped by to see if you had heard any new developments about Curtis and the mayor's nieces," he said.

"Well, yes, I have. Come on back and we'll sit and have a good ole chinwag," she teased.

Cora busied herself making them each a cup of hot cocoa while Ollie made himself comfortable in his usual wingback chair. Ollie visited Cora often, and their talks were most precious to him. She's so like her mother, he thought.

"This is going to be a long one, but don't worry about us getting interrupted. I'll see them on my phone," she said.

"On your phone? What in the dickens are you talking about?" said the sweet, aging septuagenarian. Cora could see on his perfectly lined face how the years were catching up to him.

"Oh, Janice and I invested in one of those doorbell cameras. If anyone comes to the door, their picture turns up on our phones."

Ollie's picture had popped up on both Cora's and Janice's phones the instant he stepped onto the shop's porch. Janice quickly slipped out the back and quietly reentered through the front to flip the sign to Closed on the shop's door.

Cora told Ollie all the news, and then they laughed about the old days, folks they knew, and how times had changed.

"Well, I best be on my way," said Ollie, as he slowly lifted himself from his comfy chair. "I move a little slower these days when my arthritis acts up. Winters are the worst," he honestly confessed.

"Wait just a little longer...please." Carol seemed nervous as she broached a new and touchy subject. Ollie lowered himself back down, took a final swig of the cocoa, and waited patiently for Cora to begin.

Ollie noted Cora was fidgeting. *I wonder what she has to tell me?* he pondered. *I hope she isn't ill.*

"How much longer are we going to play this game?"

"Game? I don't know what you mean," said Ollie, baffled.

"Old Nora Hughes, the gossip that she was, couldn't even wait for my mother's grave to settle before she broke her neck to tell me. Made a beeline to my door one week after I laid her to rest," she continued tentatively.

Ollie remained as still as a rabbit in the midst of danger.

"After Mrs. Hughes purged her soul, or should I say stirred the pot, I began going through my mother's things to see if what she said was actually true." Her voice began to quiver. Ollie's eyes flickered, his pulse quickening.

"I found a letter from you. One my mother kept hidden for decades."

She tried to sound casual, as her nerves prickled. A cold fear began to settle in her chest at the thought of what his reaction might be, and the possibility that the truth would shatter their friendship.

"I think you might be my father. Are you, Ollie?"

She said the last few words so tenderly and so full of hope, Ollie thought his heart would burst.

"I...I," he stammered, looking for the perfect words to tell her, but they eluded him in his desperate time of need.

"I suspected for a long time, Ollie. When I saw you at the funeral and at the gravesite, you looked as forlorn as I felt. And, if I'm guessing correctly, this was the blackmail that Curtis and James were using against you to force you to vote for the new project. Mrs. Hughes must have told Curtis. How else would he have known?"

Cora peered into his eyes, longing for the secret that had haunted her since childhood to be revealed.

"Yes, it's true," Ollie said so softly she barely heard him, but, at last, she knew the truth. It was in his eyes, and she finally drew a breath of relief.

"There's just so much to tell you," he responded. "So very much."

"Let me call Janice to come watch the store, and we can take our time. Please, I've waited a lifetime."

As Janice returned through the front entrance, she quietly closed the backroom door and let the story be told and the tears flow.

***

Elizabeth and her daughters had a holiday adventure every day leading up to Christmas, and all were as happy as larks. She and her beloved twins went Christmas shopping in nearby Mapleville, where the girls secretly purchased their mother a very special Christmas gift. They then strolled by the lake and watched the amateur ice skaters slide and tumble, laughing at their antics, as they sipped hot cider. They watched a few Harry Potter movies and spent a wonderful evening at the Sugar Bowl, being spoiled and coddled by their elderly aunts. One day, they spent the entire afternoon browsing and purchasing books from the Bibliophile and laughing their heads off at Peg's hilarious stories.

Elizabeth looked for Finch at the Cupboard, but he must have been off that day. She was so wrapped up in seasonal joy that she'd hoped to see him to spread a bit of holiday cheer. She even wanted him to meet her daughters. Then she gasped, frozen in mid-thought, blinking in surprise. Where in the world did those thoughts come from? Maybe she was warming up to the old geezer after all. The banter was fun, she had to admit.

But the days were brimming with Christmas bliss, her daughters were home, and, well, time seemed to speed by until Finch slowly became an afterthought.

***

Christmas had at last arrived with all the pomp and glory the season promised. Presents abounded under the tree, and mother and daughters oohed and ahed as the scent of fresh pine wafted about the room. The last surprise was yet to be presented. It was a small box wrapped in satiny white paper, gleaming in gold Christmas ribbon.

"Mom, this is your last present," beamed Eva.

"We can't wait for you to open it!" squealed Ava, flapping her hands like a clumsy bird, nearly bouncing off the floor with the sheer force of her happiness.

"Oh my, it's so beautiful I hate to unwrap it," teased Elizabeth. "But...I will!" she added, as she gently undid the intricate wrapping.

The twins stood beside her, buzzing with holiday anticipation, hands entwined and wearing grins so wide it seemed they might tip over from joy alone.

Elizabeth gingerly opened the gift and looked inside the deep-blue velvet casing. "Oh, my goodness! Lying in the plush cushioning was a brooch of such quality that it literally gleamed. As she picked it up to inspect it closer, she found herself absolutely dumbfounded. "Where in the world did you find this?" she whispered, hardly able to speak or believe what she saw.

"We had it specially ordered when we were home last summer. Mr. Lloyd promised it would be here in plenty of time for

Christmas." Ava was so overjoyed at her mother's reaction that she almost did a set of jumping jacks right in front of the tree.

"We stopped in to see it when we went to Mapleville and were thrilled with it. We had him wrap it for us so you couldn't snoop and find it," said Eva, with a glint of mischief in her eye.

There in Elizabeth's aging hands was a perfect replica of Abner. His head and body were decked out in tri-colored gems, and there was a bright red collar that glistened around his neck. "This is perfect."

"You always wore a pin on your suits when you taught, and we thought it was time you added to your collection," beamed Ava, so proud of the gift that totally dazzled their mother.

"Do you like it?" asked Eva.

"This is the most magnificent thing I've ever seen. I love it so much," said Elizabeth, as tears welled in her eyes. "It looks just like my boy." The one I almost lost, she thought.

After more hugs and tears, the threesome gathered the remaining gifts and set off to Beryl's, where the holiday feast awaited.

Elizabeth found herself tingling with anticipation at seeing her family and sharing this holiday with her daughters. It seemed that all was right with the world. Why, she was even looking forward to seeing her friendly nemesis, and if she were honest, she missed the old seasoned sourpuss with his pompous attitude and grandstanding techniques.

Bill and Beryl's white, old-fashion two-story home sat handsomely on a hill, offering a picturesque view of the lake. The yard was always impeccably mowed, and lush flowers in a myriad of colors bloomed from spring through late fall. Majestic pillars framed the front of the house, adorned with colorful lights, while towering 10-foot nutcrackers stood like sentinels at the entryway. It had "Merry Christmas" and "Welcome" written all over it.

The Evans clan was met at the door by a barrage of relatives, waiting to give affectionate hugs and greetings. Jack and Bill welcomed them into the festive fray. "My crew is going to be late," informed Peg, but they're on their way." Beryl's brood returned to the kitchen, helping with the food prep, setting the table, and laying out the drinks. It was a gleeful atmosphere. As was the Morgan way, everyone made it home to feast on an old Welsh tradition of Christmas goose and oyster dressing with all the fixings. Tantalizing smells wafted from the oven as the dishes were transported to the table.

"Where's Ollie?" questioned Peg, as she looked about the room. "I thought for sure he would have been here by now. He's never late for Beryl's Christmas dinner."

"Oh, he called a couple of days ago," said Beryl, through the hustle and bustle of putting all the goodies on display. "He's having his dinner at Cora Roberts's this year."

"Cora's?" said Grace incredulously, wondering if she misheard.

"Why in the world would he go over there?" questioned Peg, a tad disappointed at not seeing her old friend. "He always comes here."

"Mmm, who knows?" mused Grace, wondering if her hunch were right. "Christmas does strange things to people. I'm sure he'll have a good time. Cora's quite entertaining."

"And where's Finch?" asked Elizabeth, as inconspicuously as she could. "Don't tell me he bailed on Beryl's cooking and another free meal."

"Actually he called yesterday. Apparently something important came up last minute, and he had to go out of town. He said to tell everyone, 'Merry Christmas,' puffed Beryl, as she hustled to and from the kitchen with a flush across her cheeks.

"Out of town? I thought he didn't have any family. That's strange. Now where do you suppose he's gone off to?" pondered Elizabeth.

"Oh, are you missing him?" whispered Grace.

"Absolutely not! Let the old curmudgeon make someone else's holiday miserable," Elizabeth said with a dismissive wave as she made her way to the kitchen. But not before Grace shot her a look that was unmistakable. She didn't believe a word of it.

***

As the last dishes were dried and the floor swept, all those who attended Beryl and Bill's Christmas feast gathered around the old-fashioned tree and sang "Hark the Herald Angels Sing," as Peg's granddaughter played the piano, and the younger ones distributed gifts.

"Beryl, that dinner was amazing. I ate way too much," Jack groaned, patting his stomach.

"Oh, Jack, I told you to stop after that last helping of dressing," Peg said, scolding him good-naturedly.

"Looks to me like you loved it a little too much yourself," Jack teased, just before getting an elbow in his side. His cheeks turned crimson as he laughed and laid a kiss upon her cheek, enjoying the familiar antics of his partner for over fifty years.

"Bill, what did you get for Christmas?" asked Grace. She was so very fond of Bill, one of the kindest men she had ever known.

He had wholeheartedly agreed to let their beloved mother come live with him and Beryl when she was no longer able to live alone. Seren Jones Morgan, the proud matriarch of this distinguished old Welsh family, could not have received better care anywhere else in the world. Bill made certain she knew, beyond a shadow of a doubt, that their home was now her home.

Grace would always hold a special place in her heart for this wonderful human being. She let herself reflect on the generosity of her sister and brother-in-law, remembering what good people they were and how proud she was to be part of such a remarkable family.

"Too much," replied Bill, shaking Grace from her reverie.

"Children get too much these days," added Beryl. "When we were growing up, we each got an apple in our sock and were grateful for it. In the fall, we buried all the apples from our tree so they wouldn't go bad. We didn't have refrigeration back then."

"No refrigeration!" gasped Eva. She well knew this story, but wanted it told once again this Christmas.

"Yes, and they always tasted like dirt, but oh, how I'd love to have one of those apples now! Nothing tastes as good as a Christmas morning apple," said Peg, revisiting her youth with a wistful smile.

"Don't forget the peanuts! We always had peanuts in our stockings, too!" piped Grace.

"And if you were *really* lucky..." said Ava.

"We got an orange, too!" finished Beryl. "But that was rare!"

"That's why Mom always gives us those same treats in our stockings," said Ava.

"They'll always get an apple, peanuts, and an orange in their socks from me," Elizabeth said with a smile.

"Just like this year," added Ava.

"And we promise to carry on this tradition when we have kids," Eva said emphatically.

"Of course you will," said Grace fondly.

As the snow fell and coats and scarves were donned, each would return to their homes and quietly relive those enchanting childhood memories all wrapped up in yet another magical Morgan Welsh Christmas.

***

Somewhere in a small, elegant dining room, Finch was finishing his Christmas dinner. As plates were cleared, he leaned across the starched white tablecloth and spoke very softly to his comrade. "Thank you for coming."

"Not at all, Mr. Finch. I was not looking forward to more drama over the Christmas turkey." She frowned briefly, remembering volatile holidays that had her shying away from any future family gatherings. "I understand this matter needs immediate attention."

"Unfortunately, the timing couldn't be worse, but, then again, it couldn't be helped. I know you understand this needs to be done out of the public eye. That's why I had to leave North Falls and come here. This is very important to me, Ana, and I need your complete discretion.

"You can count on me, Mr. Finch."

"I completely trust you and those amazing skills you have with that computer of yours." The elderly judge smiled at his young protege, realizing just how fortunate he was that their paths had crossed.

"You asking me to help means everything." She shyly lowered her eyes and continued. "Thank you for this delicious meal. I haven't had anything this good since we ate roast pork at the Sugar Bowl, minus the linen and candles." She smiled at the memories of the riveting investigation and her prodigious contribution in solving the case. She relished the praise that was set upon her by a group of friends who were as close as any family she had ever known. She was fiercely loyal to them all, especially

Finch, who had a true understanding of her technological proficiency.

Ana would never divulge Finch's secret and was intensely proud he had entrusted her with this project. She vowed she would do him proud.

"It is my pleasure, Ana. I wanted to show you my appreciation." And with that, they rose and got straight to the task at hand.

As he made preparations for the dreaded encounter that he could no longer ignore, Finch had immeasurable faith that Ana would find his target. He let his mind wander for just a moment. It wasn't thoughts of an unwanted confrontation that whirled about in his head, but thoughts of a retired schoolteacher that had somehow stolen his hardened heart and urged him to face a very unpleasant past.

***

As Grace, Elizabeth, Ava, and Eva headed out into the twilight from the holiday festivities, Grace whispered softly to her sister. "We got the bad guys, didn't we, Elizabeth? I wonder what Mom would have thought."

"That was quite the escapade, and really too dangerous for us to have gotten so involved. She would probably have skinned us alive," snickered Elizabeth. "But the Dolman girls will be put away, and Curtis got his just desserts for insurance fraud and pushing that project to bail him out. Actually, Grace, when you think about it, we did pretty well for amateurs."

"I wish Ana could have made it for dinner, but she already had plans. I can understand that. Everyone wants to be home with their families this time of year," said Grace dreamily.

"We were hoping to meet Mr. Finch," interrupted Eva. "We're glad Mom has made a new friend. Aren't we, Ava?"

"Now, hold on, *friend* may be stretching it a bit," said Elizabeth, a little too fervently.

Grace tried to keep a straight face. "I wonder why he cancelled? I was hoping he would come. We had such fun, girls. It was like we were the Thursday Murder Club!"

"I have no idea where he is. One would think that the old codger would've had enough decency to let us know. Calling Beryl at the last minute was rude and unappreciative of her generous invitation," said Elizabeth, as they stopped in front of Grace's lovely abode. "Men. You just can't rely on them!"

Grace hugged her nieces and bade them good night. "Merry Christmas," she sang as she disappeared inside, with no one waiting to share her evening. Within seconds, her bright holiday lights sprang to life.

"We've got another Harry Potter movie to watch. Who's in for popcorn and hot chocolate later?" suggested Elizabeth.

"We are!" said the twins, and off they went, arm-in-arm, down the tranquil street toward home and a lonely beagle, as soft snowflakes began to, once again, cover the sidewalks of North Falls.

Acknowledgements

I have been blessed with an amazing array of friends, students, colleagues, and even strangers, who have supported me throughout my journey to, at last, write my own book. Thank you.

To the stranger in Gatlinburg who walked up to me out of the blue and said, *"Why don't you just write the damn book!"* thank you for that startling jolt. That was the moment I knew a book was in my future. I hope you find this novel one day and recognize that you were the boost I needed.

To my lovely students and colleagues, thank you for believing in me and encouraging me to write. You know who you are. I love you all.

To my many friends who were so positive and pledged to buy the book even before it was finished, your enthusiasm meant the world to me. It was the icing on my "Christmas cake."

To my husband Ted

Thank you for your pep talks. Your encouragement and unwavering positivity meant the world to me. You were right, I did it!

To my amazing identical twin daughters, Katie and Chrise

You starred in so many roles in the creation of this book: editors, social media marketing team, content creators, designers, and so much more. How do I ever express how truly blessed I am to have you in my life? I couldn't have done this without you.

Katie and Chrise, you are my heart.

I have a special place in my soul for identical twins; therefore, Eva and Ava were created to bring joy and light to this story, just as my own twins have brought immeasurable joy to my earthly journey.

Although this is a work of fiction, the Morgan sisters' characters were inspired by my Welsh grandmother, Beryl Morgan McNerlin, and her remarkable sisters: Peg, Grace, and Avenel. Their warmth, humor, and love for life left a lasting, magical imprint on me. In honoring their memory, I've woven their spirit and joy throughout these pages, creating fictional, imaginative layers that shaped the plot, setting, and characters for this festival holiday novel. Our family did, in fact, immigrate to Centerville, now known as Thurman, Ohio, in the 1800s. While North Falls is a fictional town, it is lovingly based on that original Welsh settlement.

Their mother, Elizabeth Jones Morgan, (Seren in the novel) lost her own mother when she was just eight years old. As the eldest child, all the responsibility of the household fell on her tiny shoulders. (She weighed just 98 pounds her entire adult life.) Her strength and spirit made her a tremendous influence on both her family and the Welsh community.

Because of this remarkable family and their golden outlook on life, I was reared with strong Welsh values that I have cherished and passed down to my daughters.

And yes, the stocking fruit story is absolutely true.

So here it is. I hope you enjoy the venture and continue to visit the Morgan sisters in North Falls.

Happy Holidays!

About the Author

Iris Wardlow is the author of *Murder in Snowflake Village,* the first novel in the Morgan Sisters Sleuthing Club series. A retired teacher, she graduated from the University of Rio Grande (formerly Rio Grande College) and earned her master's degree from Ohio University. With a deep love for cozy mysteries and all things festive, Iris weaves her passion for storytelling into each tale, blending charm with suspense in true whodunit fashion.

When she's not writing, Iris is an avid bibliophile, spending hours lost in a good book or working on her cross-stitching projects. An animal lover at heart, she enjoys spending time with her furry companions, who often keep her company during writing sessions. A lover of the outdoors, she also enjoys long country walks that inspire the characters and plot twists in her novels

Follow Iris for updates on her next book in the Morgan Sisters Sleuthing Club series!

Instagram: @iriswardlow.writes

www.ingramcontent.com/pod-product-compliance
Lightning Source LLC
Chambersburg PA
CBHW020635260626
47157CB00008B/2751